Book Two ⌐ The Dreadhunt Trilogy

By Ross Turner

Nigel/

Congratulations!

Thanks you for entering.

Enjoy!

Ross/

Ross Turner

©Ross Turner

And perhaps when all seems lost, it may indeed be the case, if we are most fortunate, that the night is darkest before the dawn,

Only what you choose is what makes you,

I just want to be wanted,

Always,

Ross.

Chapter One

Surging across the grasslands and swarming through valleys and over ridges, Tyran's hunting party descended towards the insignificant copse and down upon their prey.

"I saw something over here!" One man shouted as he stood ahead of the rest. He raised his flaming torch in one hand whilst his other stretched out and gestured down towards the small patch of trees within which Marcii was concealed.

The flame from his torch illuminated his fiery red hair and the thick, crooked scar that ran above and around his right eye.

"Did you see the witch!?" Another voice shouted in reply, though it was not clear who the owner was, for he was lost somewhere amidst the crowd in the dim light.

"Is she there!?" A second, much deeper voice, concurred.

The man holding the torch found himself suddenly at the head of the hunt, leading the pack, with no real idea what he'd actually seen. There were no enforcers among them and somehow it seemed that his sighting of a mere shadow had earned him the right to lead.

He found himself all of a sudden the Alpha of this pack. He saw the judgement call that faced him and the many eyes upon him at such a vital moment.

Knowing that one way or another he would have to, he made a split decision.

He lied.

As is often the way in such situations.

Nonetheless, he made the right decision.

As luck would have it, his little white lie not only gained him the compliance of his men, but in fact led them directly to their prey.

Regrettably, fortune was not favouring Marcii, for although the man with the torch didn't know it, she was indeed hidden amongst the trees that he and his men were so rapidly descending upon.

But she wasn't alone.

The trees were dense and thick and the copse was too large for the hunting party to surround completely. So instead, at the command of the man with the torch and the scar, he and his men proceeded to march directly through the trees side by side, in one long, single, flat line.

He planned to flush the small forest out completely, ensuring that there was nothing left undiscovered: ensuring that Marcii could not escape.

In truth, he didn't actually expect to find her in there, for he hadn't really been convinced himself that he'd seen her in the first place.

Even as they were combing through the trees he was inventing a speech that would rally the men when they reached the other side and had found nothing.

How wrong he was.

He was hardly even concentrating when the man beside him grabbed his arm roughly.

"Do you see that?" Came the man's hissing question, his voice full of fear.

The man with the scar peered through the trees by the dim light of the moon and the stars and his flaming torch.

Scanning the woodland, he stared long and hard through the darkness, but he could see only more trees.

With the words on the tip of his tongue he was about to reply, when one of the trees seemed to move ever so slightly.

He looked on even harder.

The whole line had come to a stop, for they could all sense that something was amiss.

"What is it?" The man at his side asked, his voice quivering with fear.

But the man with the torch and the scar was trying to focus and come up with a plan.

"Quiet!" He whispered harshly in reply, and instantly the man at his side was silenced, fearful of what might be waiting for them amidst the density of the forest.

Undoubtedly the witch had used her powers to bring the very trees to life to attack them, or she had summoned some sort of foul demon to kill them and devour their souls.

Either way, whatever it was, a mountain of irrational fear rose before Tyran's men.

However, as absurd and ludicrous as their individual fears might have been, their terror as a whole was not misplaced, for indeed there was something waiting for them in the woodlands. And whilst they believed that it was either the witch Marcii, or a creation of hers, they were wrong on both counts.

It was, in fact, something infinitely worse.

Finally, it seemed the creature had waited long enough.

It advanced.

All of a sudden the blurred outline of the trees up ahead began to shift and move. It was far too late by the time the men eventually realised why.

They were not trees, they were legs, and the creature that they carried charged towards them with frightening speed. It crashed and burst through the darkness of the forest to the terrifying sound of exploding tree trunks and shattering branches.

"DEMON!!" Someone screeched.

But it was too late.

The creature made not a sound itself, but the vast noise of falling oaks echoed endlessly through the night, splitting some of the ranks of Tyran's men and almost crushing others.

Terrified screams echoed all around as chaos ensued.

Men were thrown in every direction and their shouts and cries of fear and fury were all but futile.

But, perhaps most chillingly of all, aside from the odd flicker of a shadow against their torchlight, or the sight of the very trees themselves seeming to shift and move, the men saw not a thing.

Yet they were thrown in every direction, this way and that, and trees were felled between and upon them as if they were made of straw.

It was witchcraft to be sure.

There was no other explanation.

Mayor Tyran was right.

He had always been right.

Marcii was evil.

She had to die.

But even still the creature made not a sound as it tore havoc through the ranks, which was perhaps only more terrifying.

Soon enough Tyran's men were forced to retreat.

They swept back through the trees the way they had come, fleeing for their lives.

The creature, once it saw that they were leaving, did not pursue them.

Instead, when it was satisfied that they would not return, it turned its massive bulk silently in the dark of the night and set its gaze once again upon the young, helpless Marcii Dougherty.

Chapter Two

Marcii listened to the sounds of the screams and the cries that echoed all around the copse of trees that night, seemingly amplified by the lack of light.

Strangely, the more that she listened, the calmer she became, for she was too exhausted to feel the same fear that the men did.

Something was hunting them through the darkness.

Something terrifying.

Marcii was growing more and more used to the awful concept of fear, thanks to them, so she simply lay upon the cold ground, taking in the sound of their cries all but emotionlessly.

Finally, after hearing several desperate shouts begging for retreat, the sound of their cries faded away somewhere into the distance. Marcii gathered that the creature, whatever it was, had scared Tyran's men off.

She was grateful for the quiet and closed her eyes contentedly.

If she was going to die, she would much rather die by the will of this creature, unseen and all powerful, than at the hands of Tyran's slaves.

She didn't hear movement so much as she felt it.

Curious, when Marcii opened her eyes the enormous silhouette loomed above her once more. With legs as thick as tree trunks and a monstrous body that engulfed her in its shadow, the creature was enormous.

She could still only see its outline: enough to tell that it wasn't human.

But that was plenty.

Marcii sighed and closed her eyes again, waiting for the end.

She was too terrified to feel fear.

Too exhausted to move.

She sensed the creature's confusion, but still she waited, knowing it wouldn't be long.

Sure enough, after a moment its confusion subsided and the vast being reached down to seize her.

Without a sound the creature's huge arms stretched out to grasp Marcii, surely to choke her or crush her or pummel her.

But no.

Instead, lifting her carefully up off the ground and sliding its arms beneath her body, the creature scooped Marcii up into its massive embrace, laying her gently across its forearms as if she were a delicate new born.

Marcii's breath caught and her eyes opened for a brief second, stealing a fleeting glimpse of her captor's face by the moonlight filtering down through a break in the thick canopy.

It was a sight she would never forget. Strangely, though it was far from human, the creature's black gaze filled her with a strange, soothing assurance that she simply could not describe.

Lifted high up from the ground, Marcii felt the creature rise to its full height and begin through the trees. It avoided branches and canopies silently and effortlessly, seeming to quite simply flow through the forest like water flows to the sea.

Soon it was free of the confines of the woodland and out upon the valleys and ridges. It stayed always hidden below the skyline, for its enormous bulk would have been unmissable against the now illuminated sky.

Unbelievable heat radiated from its arms and its body like nothing Marcii had ever experienced. The air was still freezing all around, but the creature's heat thawed Marcii's icy, painful body and soon sent her dozing towards sleep.

She was warm and she was comfortable. The rocking motion of the creature's pace across the plains, coupled with her exhaustion, made any chance of Marcii fending off her exhaustion futile.

The few clouds that remained above parted lazily, revealing the millennia of perfect, star spotted galaxies that always enjoy gazing down upon events such as this.

Through heavy, sleepy eyes Marcii caught fleeting glimpses of the sea of stars above her. The moon floated effortlessly amongst them and was aglow with such radiance against the pitch black blanket of the universe that it seemed most magical.

Marcii wondered for a minute if, perhaps, it was because of nights like this one that the old man Midnight stared up at the sky every night.

For a moment she was aware that they had once again passed beneath the canopy of a forest.

The creature had still not made a sound.

Her silent saviour passed from fields to forests without so much as a whisper.

But Marcii didn't know where they were, nor where they were heading, and to be perfectly honest, she didn't really care.

Finally overtaken by her exhaustion, and by the gentle rocking motion of the creature carrying her so smoothly through the night, Marcii fell into a deep, untroubled sleep.

And there she remained, entirely helpless in the enormous hands of whatever creature it was that had claimed her.

Chapter Three

Marcii's slumber did not release her willingly and for quite some time it held her tightly within its grasp, reluctant to let go.

It filled her mind with vivid thoughts and dreams and fears and memories all mixed together as one. Tyran's face flashed in and out of her vision, followed by images of his enforcers, and indeed also her fellow townsfolk of Newmarket. They brandished swords and spears and flaming torches and pitchforks, all seeking her blood alike.

Then, at the mere thought of the hunt, Marcii was faced with pictures of her family, burned alive and screaming at the stake.

The fresh, decaying smell of their burning flesh filled her nostrils once again, making her gag and heave even in her dreams.

Strangely enough though, following that, leaving a vast pit in her stomach, there came two more memories that filled Marcii's mind.

One was of Malorie, stood alone in a tower overlooking an abandoned town. Tears streamed from her perfect violet eyes and her chest heaved with every breath.

And then, looming behind Malorie, casting its enormous shadow over her, stood the creature that had captured Marcii.

Or, perhaps more accurately, the creature that had saved her.

As Malorie cried out, distraught and inconsolable, the creature took a single, monstrous step towards her. It reached forward with its huge, black hand, yearning out to her in a way Marcii had never seen.

It was eventually those unnerving images that pulled the young Dougherty from the depths of her dreams and stirred her to wake, hard as slumber may have tried to wrench her back.

The first thing Marcii felt when she awoke, before her eyes had even opened, was the incredible warmth that had sent her to sleep in the first place. It seemed to encompass her entirely, not coming from one particular direction, but rather from all around her.

Then, as she moved to open her eyes, her face brushed again something very soft that tickled her cheek. She suddenly became aware that her fingers were clutching tightly at what felt like thick fur.

It was the slow rise and fall that finally did it however, as her body lifted and sunk in gentle rhythm to the sound of deep, heavy breaths.

Startling awake all of a sudden, filled with fear, Marcii's gaze laid immediately upon the face of the creature, towering above her, cradling her in its arms.

Horror overtook her entirely, filling her so completely that she couldn't even muster a scream. She half rolled and half leapt to her feet and within seconds was darting away as fast as she possibly could, looking desperately for the exit of what she quickly realised was a cave.

The cave was wide and somehow well lit, though she was far too terrified to wonder how.

Not a moment too soon, as she fled, her escape was in sight.

Bursting from her confinement Marcii exploded from the cave mouth and out into the dense forest beyond. Fresh, cold air hit her like a brick wall.

Without a thought her legs carried her off into the trees, wholly prepared to run until once again they could no longer move.

However, after a few more seconds, slowing to a walk and brushing the bark of the trees and the leaves of the shrubs with her hands, Marcii found herself for some reason having second thoughts.

She was doubting her natural human instinct to run.

There was something nagging in the depths of her mind, pulling her back.

She couldn't place it, but whatever it was, it was strong enough to halt her petrified flight in its tracks.

At first she didn't turn back, for her mind was too filled with flitting thoughts to make a decision. But she couldn't settle on a single notion, for they whipped in and out of her mind like frantic butterflies, never settling.

Marcii could see through the canopy of the trees that the sun was just about to clear the horizon. It's cold, orange glow looked inviting and peaceful, but it reminded her all too keenly of the chills that crept over her skin, for the morning was not blessed with warmth and she had goose bumps crawling all over her.

All of a sudden, unbelievably, she missed the cave.

She missed its heat and its security.

An abrupt, insatiable curiosity swelled and grew inside of her. She longed suddenly to know more of the creature that resided within.

She wanted to know the creature that had saved her.

Turning slowly, scanning the dense trees with quick, darting eyes as she went, Marcii could not see the cave. It was so well hidden, down a ditch and right at the base of a tree, that it was virtually impossible to find if you weren't looking for it. Had she not have known it was there she would likely never have stumbled across it.

Though wide, the entrance was very low and well concealed. Marcii imagined it was virtually invisible at night.

The creature had not followed her when she'd fled, though she wasn't entirely sure why.

Should it have pursued her?

Or did it know she would return and was waiting in ambush?

Stepping around the base of the tree and glancing down the slowly sloping ditch, Marcii took a very deep breath, wondering if she was making the right decision.

She may as well just take the plunge, she eventually decided. If she didn't, her burning curiosity would never have been satisfied, and that can be a burden all of its own.

Besides, what had she got to lose?

Only Kaylm, she thought immediately. Though he had likely been persuaded, if not forced, to join the hunt for her now too. If Tyran hadn't managed to turn him, then his family certainly would have.

Marcii hoped she was wrong, though she knew the odds were slim.

Still, in the face of everything, there is always hope.

Chapter Four

The cave was warm and oddly inviting. The walls were damp, likely from all the rain, and they flickered and danced with orange, glowing light that emanated from deeper towards the back of the cavern, where Marcii had first awoken.

Her footsteps echoed all around and the sound sang loudly in her ears, but still there was no sign of the creature, or any trap it had set for her return.

All of a sudden, as she stepped around a steep column of rock that had perhaps at one time been a devoted stalagmite and stalactite couple, there it was.

The young Dougherty came face to face with the creature that had brought her here in the first place, after it had saved her life of course.

It was sat at the rear of the cavern with its back pressed against the flat face of the wall.

Though it was huge as it was, Marcii imagined it would be probably over a dozen feet taller stood at full height. Its legs were thick like tree trunks, as were its arms, and they looked strong and powerful beyond belief.

It had a thick hide covered entirely in shaggy, black fur, save its face and hands and feet. They were bare of fur, though its black skin looked rugged and tough and unnervingly human.

Its face looked astonishingly human too, though it was more square. It's eyes however, as full of words and emotion as they might have been, were black as the night itself.

As Marcii stared on, unsure of what to say or do, the creature gazed back at her with an expression completely unreadable. It was as if it was trying to make its mind up on her, just as she was doing in return.

Finally, after what seemed to be a very lengthy silence, the creature leaned forward and rested its enormous knuckles on the hard, rocky floor of the cave.

Shifting its weight and lifting its legs, it rose surprisingly gracefully onto all fours, like a great ape, and crossed the dozen feet or so to where Marcii stood. She remained glued to the spot, unable to move.

There was a fire over to one side of where the creature had sat, which was where the flickering light had originated from, Marcii realised.

But, as it drew closer, even still she felt the unbelievable heat from its body, and she knew in an instant that the cave was not warm because of the fire, but because of the creature itself. The fire was simply there to provide light.

It stopped but a few feet short of her and gazed down curiously at its little guest, reading her eyes with its own deep, coal pupils.

Sliding its back legs forward, the creature lowered itself to sit again, propping itself up slightly with its arms.

Confused by its strange behaviour, Marcii at last plucked up the courage to speak, though she wasn't sure if it would understand her.

"What are you?" She asked, though her voice peaked slightly with her uncertainty.

The creature did not reply and instead it just continued to look down upon her curiously, as if all was normal.

Marcii sighed.

She shouldn't have thought it would be able to understand her.

But then the creature's expression changed, seeing her self-frustration. It frowned in a very human way and thought on Marcii's words.

That took Marcii aback slightly and she went to speak again.

But before she had a chance to the creature lifted its vast arms into the air, silencing her with its fluid movement. It wove some kind of gesture with its huge, hairless hands, its skin so thick that it looked like rough leather.

It indicated towards itself first and then traced some kind of pattern in the air that Marcii did not know.

As soon as it had finished it looked on expectantly at her, but she returned its hopeful expression blankly.

It frowned again and scratched the side of its face in a way that made it seem so unbelievably human that Marcii's stomach actually knotted.

Then it tried again, gesturing once more to itself and weaving another pattern in mid-air, this one slightly different to the last.

All of a sudden something clicked into place and Marcii drew a sharp, shocked breath. Her eyes widened and the knot in her stomach tightened endlessly.

"Reaper…?" She breathed, barely able to get the sound off her tongue.

The creature suddenly beamed, revealing rows of razor sharp, pristine white teeth and its black eyes lit up in exultation, if that were even possible.

It nodded eagerly and traced the same pattern in the air once more, indicating to itself repeatedly.

"I…" Marcii stumbled. "I can't beli…" She attempted.

The creature nodded and smiled.

"Malorie's Reaper…?" Marcii finally managed, unable to believe quite what she was hearing, or perhaps more accurately, seeing.

Reaper nodded again and smiled enthusiastically, showing once again his flawless, white teeth from between his rough, black lips.

He drew yet another pattern in the air before Marcii and once again she didn't recognise it. Nonetheless, though she had no idea how, she understood exactly what he was saying to her.

The outline his hands drew depicted that he was indeed Malorie's closest friend. And, also that he somehow knew who she was too: the young, exiled Marcii Dougherty.

Marcii swallowed nervously, afraid of what her next breath might bring. But it didn't matter the consequences. She couldn't leave him in the dark on such a thing.

"Reaper…" The young Dougherty started, though her words wavered noticeably. Reaper noticed her hesitation quite clearly.

He looked on at Marcii and raised his rough, leathery eyebrows slightly, awaiting her words eagerly.

He had been alone for so long.

She was the first person he had ever spoken to besides Malorie, and it felt like a lifetime since he'd last seen her.

"I'm so sorry Reaper…" Marcii whispered. "Malorie's dead…"

Chapter Five

Reaper closed his black eyes and exhaled deeply. His chest seemed to fall endlessly as he did so, caving in with deep thought and despair. He didn't look back at Marcii for quite some time.

When he eventually did, though the droplets were well hidden amidst the thick, leathery lines of his rough, black face, Marcii saw quite clearly the tears trickling from Reaper's eyes.

It was not the response Marcii had been expecting, but before she had chance to draw breath to reply Reaper was weaving another pattern with his huge hands.

His eyes remained closed and still he made not a sound, but his fingers told Marcii that he had already known Malorie was dead.

He knew she had been murdered.

To that, Marcii had no reply.

Suddenly she felt tears streaming down her own cheeks.

When Reaper opened his brimming eyes to look upon the young girl again, he saw that she shared in at least a little of his pain.

Marcii's legs carried her before her mind could even think and she found herself wrapping her arms around Reaper, or at least as much of his massive body as she could manage. She buried her head into his thick, warm, soft fur and the heat from his enormous bulk engulfed her.

He seemed surprised at first, but then pleased. He lifted one arm and carefully laid it around Marcii, ensuring he didn't hurt her.

After a few minutes the young Dougherty stepped back and craned her neck back to look up at him.

He wiped his eyes dry and looked down at her, his jet black irises filled with sorrow.

His hands came up and danced in front of his chest, asking if Marcii had known Malorie well.

"She was my friend." Marcii replied simply.

Reaper didn't need to tell her that Malorie had been more than just a friend to him, for his expression spoke volumes that mere words would never have been able to.

Somehow Reaper could convey perfectly everything he wanted to say without the need for speech. His seemingly limitless expressions and gestures, combined with his body language, allowed his conversation with Marcii to grow and flourish.

She struggled sometimes to pick up what he was trying to say, but soon enough she understood him easily. It didn't take long for them become perfectly in tune with one another.

Reaper asked Marcii if she wanted to rest some more. He told her that the men would not find them here and that they were safe in the cave.

But although Marcii was tired, exhausted in fact, she could not sleep while she had so many questions. Her mind buzzed with activity and Reaper could see that her eyes were bright and inquisitive. He saw that her gaze was luminous and full of life, much in the way Malorie's had always been, and his heart filled with sorrow once again.

It showed not on his face however, for he didn't let it escape his control.

Marcii needed to ask at least one or two more questions to satisfy her burning curiosity.

"Have you always lived here?" She asked of Reaper then, cocking her head slightly to one side and glancing briefly around the cave.

He gestured with his hands a simple and remorseful motion: mostly.

"Why?" She asked immediately, without thinking. Instantly though she regretted it and wished she could take back her foolish question.

The answer to her query was all too obvious as she looked upon the vast, terrifying, gentle creature sat before her.

"I'm sorry…" She breathed.

Nonetheless, Reaper's hands set about replying. They wove a complex and intricate pattern with deft, enormous fingers, forming shapes and outlines perfectly for the young Dougherty.

He told Marcii of how all feared him, although they did not know him. He explained that the only person he'd never had to hide from was Malorie. And now that she was gone, he would only ever be known as a demon.

"Reaper…" Marcii whispered, though her very breath oozed with guilt at his name, for it had been she who had revealed him to Newmarket in the first place.

She had named him as a demon, and then in fact, even unwillingly, she had led them right to him.

He had saved her life, both from the hunting party and from the elements, and she had offered him only betrayal and fear and interrogation in return.

Her body racked with guilt.

"I'm so sorry…" She repeated for the third time. "This is all my fault…"

But Reaper shook his head adamantly, almost as if he could sense her every thought.

He told her not to apologise, as his hands and fingers danced for her still.

Ogre.

Demon.

Giant.

Monster.

Reaper motioned to Marcii how he had been called every name under the sun, and that they all meant the same thing. He told her that they were just names that men gave their fears, to turn them into enemies.

He explained how he thought that men did it because it made them feel better: that they would be less afraid if they were facing some creature in particular, and not simply a nameless enemy.

Even if that creature was a made up fantasy, it didn't matter.

The ideas Reaper wove astounded Marcii and she couldn't help but be drawn into them.

She couldn't help but believe them, for they made perfect sense.

He was not wrong.

It was a childish act, to be sure.

To justify fear by inventing a monster of some kind: ghosts, bogeymen, ghouls, werewolves, vampires.

They were all simply figments of imagination.

It seemed all of a sudden obvious to Marcii that it was a habit children didn't grow out of, and in fact, it was something that only worsened as they got older, as their imaginations grew wilder and more experienced.

Reaper had indeed opened her heart, for he looked at the world she had lived in for her whole life through completely different eyes.

It didn't take much for Marcii to decide that she liked the way he looked at the world.

He was like nothing she'd ever known.

Marcii hoped she would come to know him, for indeed he was all she could ever have asked for and more.

Chapter Six

Marcii rested for most of what remained of the day. The night had been long and exhausting and soon enough her fatigue got the better of her.

Reaper knew that when she awoke, though she might have been rested, she would be hungry.

He assured her that once dusk had passed and night had fallen, they would hunt.

He could not go out during the day, for when it was light he had no way to conceal himself from the fearful, prying eyes of men.

There were still many questions that floated around in Marcii's thoughts as she settled once again into Reaper's warm lap to sleep, but there was one more prudent and more at the forefront of her mind than all the rest.

And so, as slumber once again reared its head to claim her, Marcii thought on the question that Reaper himself had raised in her mind. When he'd told her that people had called him a demon, a monster, even a giant, Marcii had gotten to wondering a few things.

Where had he come from?

How had he come to know Malorie?

But most of all, if not an ogre or a monster or a giant, what was he?

She was adamant however, above all else, that he was no demon, for he was kinder and more gentle than most people she had ever known.

She wasn't about to ask him those things though. She was afraid enough that she'd already hurt his feelings and so she kept her questions to herself, allowing sleep to carry her off for what was left of the day.

It didn't take long.

The night had most certainly drained her.

The sounds of the surrounding stone and of the woodlands outside soothed her as they echoed endlessly around the cave. It seemed that the rock and earth was just as alive and made just as much noise as the creatures that chirped and barked and hummed amidst the trees.

Reaper cradled Marcii gently, just as he had done when he'd rescued her.

He looked down upon the sleeping girl curled in his lap with both kindness and affection. Such emotions he was full of, but he hadn't been able to share them for such a long time.

Solitude had been all he'd known for so many long years now.

He had always loved Malorie and, naturally, cared very deeply for her.

But, unfortunately, as is all too often the case, he had only been able to do so from afar. He could not have gone to Newmarket and she had been bound there by her duties.

Little did young Marcii Dougherty know of all that though, and for now at least, that would have to be the way it remained.

Chapter Seven

Marcii did not toss and turn as she slept, for she felt secure in Reaper's embrace. She rested soundly and peacefully and without being plagued by nightmares.

Eventually though, just as dusk was cast over the mountains and the fields and forests of the land, her hunger stirred her to waken, for her stomach was growling fiercely.

With a long yawn she looked up and blinked awake.

She noted curiously that Reaper seemed to be sat in exactly the same position as when she'd last looked up. He had not shifted even slightly.

The fire had been reduced to smouldering embers, for it had not been replenished, though its glow still shone the damp walls of the cave a warm amber colour.

Reaper cast his gaze down slightly and Marcii could just about make him out in the murky darkness above her, for her eyes were adjusting well to the lack of light.

"Didn't you sleep?" She asked curiously.

Because Reaper's one arm was tied up beneath her, he responded, somehow, with only his expression, a slight lift of his massive shoulders, and one huge hand, all just about visible by the dim firelight.

He explained to her with nothing more than a simple gesture, a commonplace expression, and a slight shrug, that he did not need to sleep.

He never had done.

"Really?" Marcii questioned, intrigued. "Why?"

But Reaper did not know, and he told Marcii exactly that.

The young Dougherty was finding the mysterious creature Reaper more and more fascinating by the moment. But, just as she drew breath to ask another question, her stomach rumbled a deep reminder that she was long overdue a meal.

Reaper's expression was knowing and he lifted Marcii effortlessly to her feet, whilst at the same time placing his free hand on the floor to bring himself onto all fours.

Marcii clutched at her shrinking waistline and giggled sheepishly, for the sound of her stomach's cries echoed about the cave in all directions.

With a faint gesture of his hand Reaper motioned towards the cave entrance, warning Marcii with a mere flicker of his eyes that if they did not find food soon, sleep would not be enough to restore her strength.

She didn't speak this time, but instead nodded in reply, smiling her thanks.

His concern was well noted by the young girl.

Reaper led Marcii carefully to the entrance of the cave. Even before she emerged out into the forest that she knew lay beyond she could feel the biting chill of the wind longing to cut her to shreds.

Pausing at the sloping entrance and turning to face her, concern evident in his eyes, Marcii knew what Reaper was going to ask before he'd even raised his hands.

Sure enough, as she had predicted, his motions wove a question in the dark of the night, asking her if she would rather remain there. The weather was on the turn again and it was only going to get colder.

He assured her that he wouldn't be long.

"I want to come." Marcii replied, adamant that she wanted to help in any way that she could. "I can't let you feed me and do nothing in return."

Reaper's expression was understanding, but his eyes hardened slightly as if to make his point more firmly. His hands did exactly the same as they wove again into motion, for they cut clearly and precisely through even the darkness.

He pointed out to her, and quite rightly so, that food would be no good to her if she died of cold before it was cooked. As his fingers danced he eyed the leather jacket she still wore, for though it was a fine garment, albeit filthy, it was not suited for the harshness of winter.

He made his point quite clear.

Marcii smiled and sighed.

"You're right, of course…" She admitted. "I just feel so useless…" She dropped her head and her shoulders sagged, but already she could feel the shivers of cold coming on, even just stood in the entranceway to the cave.

Reaper's enormous hand came to her chin and lifted it so that her eyes met his, and with those jet black coals he reassured her almost wholly.

Weaving yet another kindness with his fingers, he requested that she replenish and stoke the embers for his return, for the meat would not cook without fire, and better to have one ready and waiting than to have to start from scratch.

"Thank you." Marcii replied gratefully and she wrapped her arms around Reaper's enormous neck, only just about able to reach him because he was stood on all fours, and even then she had to jump.

He looped one hand softly around her back for a few moments before turning and hastening towards the entrance. The winds were howling louder by the second and undoubtedly the rains would soon follow.

"Will you be alright!?" Marcii called, concerned, having to practically shout above the wailing screeches of the elements.

Reaper clambered up and out from the entrance to the cave as Marcii looked on frightfully. After a moment however her apprehension was replaced with sheer awe and all her worries faded away.

He pushed off from the ground like a great, monstrous bear, rising up onto two feet and standing steadfast against the cruel, driving winds.

But he did not stand like a bear: hunched forward and slightly off balance.

No.

Instead he stood taller, and straighter, and broader, and infinitely more human than anything Marcii could possibly imagine.

He turned back to her and glanced down the entrance to the cave, seemingly so far below now, smiling warmly at Marcii even in the face of the freezing cold.

His arms raised and his hands spoke just as perfectly as they always seemed to, for it was surely not Marcii's doing that she understood him so easily, but undoubtedly his.

Dancing their final message before he vanished into the blackness, his enormous hands assured the young Dougherty there was no need for her to worry, for he felt not the cold, just as he needed not to sleep. He promised that she would see him again very soon.

And with those final words he was gone, replaced by the black of the night that engulfed everything it touched.

Chapter Eight

The wind had been screaming for hours and it was only getting worse. The rain had started too. It was coming down sideways and bore brutally into anything it could find.

But Kaylm didn't care.

He might not have been a dozen feet tall, almost as wide and immune to the cold, but his anger and his indifference made up for all of that tenfold as he trudged through the streets.

Tyran's hunting parties had been out most of the night but had started returning soon after the weather turned so vile. Kaylm had declined to join them. He had not voiced his refusal too loudly however, for he knew it wouldn't take much for him to find himself at the end of a rope.

Any support for Marcii, or refusal to hunt her, would have undoubtedly resulted in yet another conviction of conspiracy.

He couldn't afford that.

Not now.

Not if he was going to help her.

That's why he was out so late, braving such dire weather.

He was looking for a weakness in Tyran's troops. A chink in their armour. Anything that he could exploit to help slow down the hunt for Marcii. He had to help her in any way he could.

Though of course he wanted to aid her, really, deep down, Kaylm wanted to find her. He was lost without his young Dougherty, and more than once he'd found himself sat alone behind the vines that covered the inlet in the church walls, waist deep in lonesome thought, pining for his missing friend.

The news of the terrifying demon that Marcii had summoned to attack the hunting party had spread through Newmarket like wildfire.

He didn't believe it, naturally.

She wasn't going around consorting with demons and witches, if there even were such things.

The whole idea was simply ludicrous.

Suddenly, through the almost impenetrable wall of rain that filled the air, Kaylm spotted three figures scurrying through the night. He dove down a narrow, putrid alleyway, disappearing out of sight right at the last second.

The figures did not see him, but as they hurried past he heard the heavy jingle of their armour and smelled the stench of oil and sweat hanging behind them.

Enforcers.

The temptation to follow them and bury a knife between their shoulder blades was enticing to say the least. But, hungry for revenge though Kaylm might have been, for he was only human after all, he was no fool. He knew that although he might have brought down one of them, perhaps even two if he was lucky, he wouldn't be able to take all three.

And besides, there were so many of them now, for Tyran was bringing more and more in seemingly by the hour, that any kind of revolt would last all of but a few moments.

His wealth must have been endless and for a moment Kaylm envied the cruel man. Not for his money, but instead for his position.

A man with that much authority could do so much good in the world, and here he was squandering it for the sake of power and control.

It made Kaylm sick to the stomach.

Grunting slightly as he rose to his feet, the determined Kaylm Evans pressed on again and out into the night, off to see if he could sabotage yet another storeroom. So far two of Tyran's food stores had been mysteriously left with their doors slightly ajar, allowing all manner of vermin and cats and dogs and even hungry townsfolk to gain access to wealth of food within.

An army cannot hunt on an empty stomach, after all.

That was Kaylm's thinking at least.

Disappointingly, it seemed not to be making too much of a difference. Nonetheless, he pressed on, knowing he had to do something.

But he knew that wouldn't last. He was sharp enough to realise that soon he would have to do something drastic.

He had to find Marcii, and he would have to do so before Tyran's men did, or anyone else in Newmarket for that matter.

They all longed for the witch's blood to flow thickly through the streets.

Freezing cold water ran freely down his face and his clothes were soaked through.

He didn't know how many more hours it would be until sunrise. Probably not too many, he prayed.

Sighing and pulling his cloak more tightly around himself, out of force of habit more than anything else, for it made no difference whatsoever, Kaylm continued through the dark, lonely streets.

His mind swam with thoughts of Marcii Dougherty, and all manner of insane and ludicrous plans to stop Tyran and to save her.

Certainly every idea and notion was a guaranteed death sentence.

But Kaylm was getting to the point where he didn't care about the consequences.

He only cared about Marcii.

Just knowing she was okay would be worth it.

And so, with that heavy, burdensome thought firmly set in mind, Kaylm made his decision, knowing that one way or another he absolutely had to do something.

He didn't know how, but he would find her.

If there was such a beast as Tyran's men had described, he would kill it and rescue her and then they would run away together, just like they'd always talked about.

Kaylm sighed deeply and his shoulders slumped, the cold and the exhaustion finally breaking down his barriers.

It all just felt like wishful thinking.

Above all else, he just hoped she was still alive.

Chapter Nine

Marcii found dry firewood at the back of Reaper's cave where the rainfall could not reach and where Reaper's warmth still hung amidst the stone. Starting with smaller pieces of kindling and building up to larger chunks of wood, the young Dougherty stoked the fire back to life until it crackled and spat and roared.

Because the entrance to the cave sloped downwards from the forest above, the wide mouth acted like a chimney, funnelling the smoke upward and out into the damp air.

She could hear the wind and the rain outside still, sweeping the smoke off into the vast sky above.

It was disconcerting to listen to and, though Reaper had assured her that she didn't need to worry, Marcii frequently glanced in the direction of the cave entrance. Every so often she even paced up to the mouth to see if she could see him returning.

The rain was too thick to see very much at all and the storm had grown so fierce that Marcii daren't even poke her head out.

She had to admit, Reaper had been right. She was very glad he'd convinced her to remain.

Her stomach growled and rumbled more and more desperately by the minute. She returned hastily to keep stoking and preparing the fire. She knew somehow innately that Reaper would keep to his word and that it wouldn't be long before he returned.

Sure enough, after what felt like only a few more moments, a looming shadow appeared in the cave entrance.

Reaper slipped down from the forest above and dropped to all fours with practiced grace. He kept one hand off the floor, carrying several limp, swaying forms in his enormous grasp.

Water dripped from his fur and ran freely down his face, but it seemed not to bother him in the slightest. Even before she could see him Marcii could have sworn she felt the heat radiating off of Reaper as he approached.

"Are you okay?" The young Dougherty asked immediately, rising to her feet and stepping forward, her movements almost even involuntary.

Reaper dropped what looked to be a deer and a sheep beside the fire and lowered himself to the floor.

He gestured with his hands and his eyes that he was fine and thanked her for her concern.

Pulling the deer towards himself he looked approvingly at Marcii's fire. She smiled as he complimented her on her work and watched as he began stripping the carcass.

"Thank you." She replied. "Can I help?"

Reaper set to work expertly preparing their meal and motioned with his eyes towards the sheep. Marcii stepped around the fire to retrieve it.

All of a sudden, as she reached down to grasp it, she realised that it wasn't a catch at all, but instead sheepskin. And not only that, Marcii saw as she inspected it more closely, it wasn't raw and roughly hewn off a carcass as she'd expected.

Though it was wringing wet, it was not fresh off the sheep at all. It was perfectly cut, well cured, and the pelt was in pristine condition.

"How did you…?" Marcii began, looking up at Reaper in surprise. She knew the expense of such things and couldn't quite believe what she was holding. Their family had never been wealthy enough to know such luxuries.

Reaper looked across to her and made a string of small gestures with one hand. He told her that he knew of a farmer on the outskirts of Newmarket who cured and tanned his sheepskins into fine pelts. He was very proficient at his work and often hung them in his barn to drain and dry.

Reaper explained that whilst he could obtain a sheep and skin it, he did not have the materials to properly treat it so that Marcii could use it. And even if he had, she wouldn't have been able to leave the cave until it was finished, for the weather was growing too cold.

It would quite simply have taken too long, he concluded silently.

"You stole it?" Marcii asked, sounding perhaps more shocked than she should have been.

Reaper gestured with his hands again, stating only that it was either that or she freeze to death.

Marcii supposed that answer was reasonable enough.

"I'm sorry. Thank you." She offered, backtracking and withdrawing her shock. Reaper nodded his head in reply.

Marcii laid the pelt on a raised, outstretched section of the wall to dry and turned back to the meal Reaper was preparing.

When the meat was cooked through it was tender and almost fell off the bone before Marcii could eat it. She devoured it ravenously, realising all of a sudden exactly how hungry she was, stopping only every now and then between mouthfuls to breathe.

Reaper ate too, though he seemed not to be anywhere near as ravenous as Marcii was. Everything she did not eat, bones and all, he crunched almost negligently, as if he hadn't really been hungry in the slightest. Marcii imagined it was just another one of those things that he didn't really require, but she didn't think on it all that hard, for she was too focused on her own food.

It was only after her belly was full and stopped grumbling for more that Marcii's overactive mind once again kicked into gear.

She realised suddenly, as she wiped her mouth clean, that there was one question, perhaps most obviously of all, which she had completely neglected to even think of. As she drew breath and turned to Reaper, he looked knowingly across at her by the flickering firelight.

She could see that he was expecting it.

"Why did you save me?" Marcii asked quietly. Her words still echoed all around the wide cavern, mixing with the sound of the crackling fire.

Reaper seemed to think on her query for a moment. He gazed into the dancing heat of the flames so deeply that his coal eyes burned bright orange and red and yellow.

He raised his hands to speak, but Marcii saw almost all that he was going to say in his eyes alone.

The gentle creature told her it would not have been right to let those men kill her. He said he couldn't imagine any situation where it would be right for armed men to kill a defenceless young girl.

"They think I'm a witch." Marcii explained. "Something has been killing people in the night in Newmarket. They think I helped Malorie summon evil spirits and demons to murder people."

Reaper looked pensive for a minute.

Finally, twisting his hand with a flick of his enormous wrist, he said he supposed that now they thought he was responsible.

Marcii went white, but she could not lie to him.

"Those men in the forest will have told Tyran about you." She admitted. "Tyran is the Mayor of Newmarket now. He's the one leading the hunt for the witches. I don't think he'll let anyone, or anything, stand in his way…"

Again, Reaper did not reply immediately.

At the mention of the hunt for the witches he remained perfectly still and looked so deeply saddened that Marcii felt guilty for what she'd told him. She'd had little choice in the matter though, for she was only speaking the truth.

"When you found me…" Marcii went on, her voice little more than a whisper creeping delicately around the cave. "I'd only just escaped from Newmarket…"

Her eyes pooled deeply and Reaper looked on, expressionless and still.

"Before I escaped, I watched Tyran burn my family alive…" Now that she spoke the words Marcii felt hollow and empty inside, as if she wanted the pain to come, but it was nowhere to be found.

She took a deep, shuddering breath.

"I saw them hang people…" She continued. "Claiming it was because they were witches. They tortured Maloric and then drowned her in the river…"

Reaper saw the empty pain in Marcii's eyes and for a moment they just held each other's gaze. By the flickering firelight the young Dougherty could see the understanding in the black coals of Reaper's face, telling her without even the slightest movement that none of this was her fault.

Looking back, he could see the loss she felt, and indeed he did understand it, for he had experienced it himself.

Marcii fell suddenly into the enormous creature's arms and shuddered terribly. He cocooned her in his grasp as gently as he could manage. She clutched at his thick, shaggy fur and felt his warmth encase her. Unable to cry, for she felt so overwhelmed, Marcii just lay there for a few minutes, trying desperately to catch her breath.

Eventually, once she had settled, though she did not move, Marcii spoke again. She breathed her words through Reaper's fur, for her head was buried deep in his enormous chest and her eyes were closed.

"I was going to Ravenhead." She told him. "When you found me, I was going west." Silence followed and there was nothing but the sound of the popping fire and the screeching wind for a few minutes.

However, little did Marcii know that Reaper's thoughts were screaming at the mention of the abandoned town.

He remained motionless and silent, as he always did, but his mind cried out in terrible anguish as the memory of dreadful loss flooded through his vast body.

Ravenhead was perhaps the only human settlement he did indeed know well, for though he was not responsible for the attacks in Newmarket, Marcii's words had brought back feelings and memories he had never again wished to experience.

It was abandoned for a reason.

Chapter Ten

Over the following weeks Reaper taught Marcii the ways of the forests and the plains and indeed of the wilderness itself.

During the day they rested in the sanctuary of Reaper's cave. Well, that is to say Marcii slept, whilst Reaper sat. He could remain entirely motionless for hours and hours on end it seemed, with or without Marcii curled up on his lap.

It was only during the darkest hours of the night that they ventured out for fear of being found by one of Tyran's many hunting parties.

The air was so bitterly cold now winter had fully taken hold that Marcii daren't even venture to the mouth of the cave without wearing the sheepskin pelt Reaper had retrieved for her. It was, by no stretch of the imagination, an absolute godsend. Without it she surely would have succumbed to frostbite or pneumonia weeks ago.

The winds raked across the fields and around the sloping hills and though they did not yet carry snow with them, the screeching squalls were icy and bitter and cruel.

Marcii often thought of Ravenhead, though of course she didn't know the pain that it caused Reaper, for he did not disclose those memories to her.

She wanted to leave, to get away from Newmarket for good. Most importantly though, she wanted Reaper to come with her.

But he warned her that, for now at least, it was too dangerous to travel so far.

Although that was, admittedly, only part of the reason.

He imagined the time would eventually come when they would have no choice but to leave.

Fortunately, that time was not yet nigh.

Nonetheless, Tyran had many men combing the hillsides. Even when Reaper and Marcii were out for barely a few hours, every night they came far too close to being found.

It was surely only by some miracle that they had not yet been discovered, for every time they somehow managed to find cover to allow the hunting parties to pass. The young Dougherty often found herself mere feet away from Tyran's troops as they skulked around in the darkness.

"How do you always see them?" Marcii whispered to Reaper one night, just as they were crossing back through the forest and towards the cave with their spoils.

Reaper indicated towards his eyes in the dim light and made a small gesture with his one free hand that Marcii could only just about make out in the night. Her eyes had spent the past weeks adjusting to the impenetrable darkness that fell upon the land once the day had passed. Yet, even still she struggled desperately to see all that Reaper seemed to be able to.

"You can see the daylight?" She questioned, not entirely sure what he'd meant.

Marcii was becoming most accomplished, fluent even, in the limitless gestures and expressions that Reaper used to communicate with her. But every now and then, especially in the dead of night, when it was nearly impossible to see much more than mere silhouettes, she often had to think twice.

He repeated the motion he'd made with his hand, slowing it down and emphasising it more clearly.

"Oh!" Marcii realised, though she was careful to keep her voice hushed. "You can see as if it were daylight!"

Reaper nodded, smiling in the blackness, but Marcii's face melted from realisation into confusion.

"How…?" She questioned, baffled at the thought.

Reaper halted their pacing through the dense trees and dropped the deer he had been carrying in his right hand. He knelt so that he was almost Marcii's height and used both his hands to explain it to her.

He told her that her eyes needed light to see: that was the same for all humans. That's why people's eyes are all different colours. No matter whether they're green or blue or yellow or violet, they all needed light by which to see.

He explained how it didn't matter if that light came from the sun or the moon or the stars, or from fire or candles or lanterns, as long as there was light of some kind, she would be able to see.

Marcii nodded, amazed at what he was telling her, for she had never heard an explanation like it. She wondered how in the world he had come to know such things.

The lighter it was, the better she would be able to see, he went on. So by day, because the sun was brighter than anything else, she would see better. But by night, because the moon only reflects the light from the sun, and so was only half as bright, she would not see anywhere near as well.

"How do you see so well then?" Marcii questioned, and Reaper's hands wove his explanation continuously without stopping.

Because his eyes were black, Reaper continued to tell her, they didn't need light by which to see. He could see just as well by night as he could by day, for his eyes saw everything regardless.

"That's incredible…" Marcii breathed. "How do you know all this?" She asked.

But for that question, as simple as it might have seemed, Reaper did not have such an impressive answer.

He admitted to Marcii that he wasn't sure how he knew, gesturing to her with one hand as he picked up the deer with the other.

They turned back towards the cave, only a hundred feet or so away now, and he made a single, final gesture with a flick of his enormous wrist and a flurry of movement from his fingers.

It was just the way he was made.

Chapter Eleven

The weeks progressed in much the same way as they had been.

Marcii and Reaper crept around through the long, dark, cold nights and in turn Tyran's hunting parties combed endlessly through the hills and the forests looking for them.

Reaper taught Marcii to hunt and to skin deer and sheep and to cook entire carcasses. His knowledge seemed to be limitless and Marcii learned so much from the mysterious, kindly creature that she couldn't quite believe it.

However, there were things that Marcii began to learn that Reaper could not have taught her. They were things that she hadn't been expecting, and indeed too that she didn't understand.

The first time it happened, it came as quite the shock.

Fortunately, having already hunted that night, Reaper and Marcii had just returned from the forests and the fields and were about to settle and cook the game that was the fruit of their efforts.

Marcii knelt to tend to the fire that she'd left burning before they'd departed to hunt, adding more kindling and more logs to feed it.

She stood up to turn to Reaper, drawing breath to speak, when the feeling took her completely by surprise.

Her vision blurred and went hazy as she turned. Her head spun horribly and forced her to lurch forwards, throwing her completely off balance, as if the world itself was trembling and shaking.

The cave seemed to go black all around her and for a few moments Marcii couldn't hear or see a thing.

Terrified and blind, she cried out as she fell. Reaper only just managed to catch her before she stumbled headlong into the blazing flames.

Marcii barely even felt him save her though, for her head still spun and her vision was blurred at best.

And then, for some reason, as she felt her sight starting to return, she saw rain and buildings and streets stretched out before her.

The roads were narrow and cobblestoned and the water ran spiritedly down the long cracks and indents in the ground, leading off and into the distance in every direction.

Marcii was back in Newmarket.

Though it was into the early hours of the morning, her eyes were well accustomed to such dim scenes by now and she recognised the sight before her in an instant.

What in the world was happening?

A chill wind whipped through the dark streets, whistling as it burst between the narrow, packed in buildings, rattling doors and window frames as it went. But for some reason, although Marcii could see it scooping up scattered leaves and shaking the branches of trees, she could not feel it pass by.

Suddenly, hurrying into view at one end of the street, a figure appeared from around the corner. The man emerged and raced towards Marcii without even pausing to look where he was going.

Too stunned to react, Marcii didn't even move.

She hardly even registered what she saw.

It was only as the figure barged into her, and then yet passed straight through her, without her feeling a thing, that her mind finally started to catch up.

She turned to watch the man disappear up the dark street and around yet another corner. He sheltered his head from the fierce wind and the heavy rain as he went. The wind and rain that she could not feel.

Marcii's eyes grew yet wider with fright.

Then she heard shouts of defiance, followed by shrill screams of terror. As she turned to look back down the street, from around the same corner that the man had first appeared a dozen of Tyran's enforcers followed.

Between them they were half dragging and half carrying two women. Marcii felt a strong pang of regret and anger in her chest, for she knew all too well what that felt like.

Any enforcers that were not restraining the two terrified victims marched ahead carrying burning torches, lighting the way as if they were following a path of almighty righteousness.

The two women were not old. In fact, they were perhaps only a few years older than Marcii herself. They looked much alike too and both had long, flowing black hair and lovely brown eyes, even though their gazes were, at that moment, filled with almighty dread.

They knew what was coming to them.

And sure enough Tyran's enforcers dragged them, kicking and screaming, past Marcii and up towards the square.

Although Marcii had regained her wits enough to step out of the way this time, the enforcers hauled the two poor girls past the young Dougherty without noticing her.

It was as if she wasn't even there.

A bawling crowd followed closely behind, surging through the streets and forcing past Marcii relentlessly. Some of them were shouting their own disapproval, and for a moment, when she heard it, Marcii felt a flicker of hope ignite inside of her.

But for the most part, all but extinguishing that desperate flame, the people of Newmarket cheered and chanted and roared their support. They followed Tyran's enforcers with burning torches of their own, heading to the square to celebrate the two witches' execution.

Marcii couldn't bear to watch.

She turned her back on the lot of them and began slowly walking away, heading instinctively in the direction of Reaper's cave.

If this was to be their fate, she wanted nothing to do with these sick people ever again.

But then, as she turned to leave, turning her gaze away from the crowds, Marcii's eyes fell upon a sight that turned her stomach and melted her heart.

It was very dark still and this figure of a man did not carry a burning torch to light his way.

But that didn't matter.

Even though she could hardly see his face, Marcii knew in an instant who it was.

Kaylm.

He was there, at the bottom of the street where the enforcers and the crowds had first appeared.

Looking after him, even in the dim light, Marcii could see his eyes were filled with endless disappointment. He shook his head slowly and turned away from the sight in disgust.

He hadn't joined the hunt!

And Marcii could tell, simply by the repulsed look on his face, that he most certainly would not be persuaded.

He was still with her!

"Kaylm!" She cried.

Her heart leapt as he began to walk away. She staggered forwards toward him, but even though he turned back, seemingly on a whim, and looked on for another few moments longer, he did not hear her.

He turned away again and disappeared around the corner.

Marcii chased after him desperately.

"KAYLM!!" She screamed, but again her words went unheard. Tears streamed from her eyes and flooded down her cheeks.

But he did not respond.

As Marcii careered round the corner after him she very nearly went crashing to the floor, for her head spun terribly again and threw her completely off balance.

"NO!" She cried in futile denial, trying desperately to keep sight of her Kaylm.

But it was of no use.

She could not see.

She could not focus.

Her head whirred and spun awfully and she felt sick to the stomach, totally off balance, lurching this way and that.

Then all of a sudden Marcii felt a strong, enormous hand around her waist, steadying her as her legs gave way and she very nearly tumbled to the floor.

As she slowly opened her eyes it was still another minute or so before her spinning head calmed enough for her to see straight. When it eventually did, with tears still streaming down her face and desperate anger and longing still coursing through her veins, Marcii laid eyes immediately upon Reaper.

His expression was distorted with concern and worry.

The young Dougherty fell immediately into his arms and wept.

He didn't know what had just happened, or what she'd just seen, but he could sense her grief, although she couldn't speak of it just yet, for she was far too distraught.

The enormous, powerful, gentle creature simply held his dear Marcii closely and allowed her grief to run its course, and not for the first time either.

To the sound of once again defiant, hammering rain and distraught, screaming winds echoing from outside of the cave, Marcii sobbed until she could cry no more, and shook until she was exhausted.

The firelight that warmed the damp walls flickered and danced until it had burned itself out, but Marcii did not notice, for there were too many other thoughts filling her troubled mind.

But no matter how long or how hard the young Dougherty thought on all that she had seen and done, she came no closer to the answers that she so desired.

She longed to leave; she had to get to Ravenhead.

That much, at least, was clear.

She had been planning to speak to Reaper about it again that very night.

But after what she'd just seen, she couldn't bring herself to do it.

Instinctively, maybe even subconsciously, Marcii knew there was still more to happen.

And besides, now that she knew he was still with her, she simply couldn't bring herself to leave Kaylm.

Chapter Twelve

Foul curses ripened the air and turned it a horrible shade of blue that hovered around the breakfast table like an obscene smell.

Not to mention the disgusting stench that actually did still pervade every home on every street for miles around, for the massacred cats still had not been removed. Their remains had grown putrid and vile beyond the point of necessity. Nonetheless, Tyran still claimed they were working, for there had still not been another attack.

Kaylm winced almost visibly with every harsh word thrown in his direction, which was, unfortunately, most of them. He thought that he might have grown accustomed to it by now, but the abuse had only worsened over the last few weeks. Every time he thought he could take it, his family stepped up a gear and threw him yet ever harsher insults and threats, voicing their opinions all too clearly.

They had always been blunt.

That was the polite way of putting it at least.

But lately Tyran's hold on them had grown past the point of insanity. Kaylm feared that they would follow the man anywhere now: even to the brink of death and beyond.

"Kaylm!" His mother, Victoria Evans, barked at him when he did not respond immediately to her.

Her voice didn't have the love for Kaylm in it that Marcii's had done, only two nights previous when she'd called out to him in the darkened

Newmarket streets. But of course he didn't know that, for he had not heard her desperate cries, since she had not really been there.

"Sorry mother…" Kaylm instantly replied, keeping his voice low, for he knew that regardless of what he said or didn't say, he would not win.

He couldn't do right for doing wrong.

Of course, as his mother berated him, his father Stephen, and his older brother Malcolm, were at the table too.

He was grateful though, if he was honest, when his mother gave him grief such as this, for he knew it would always be much worse coming from Stephen or Malcolm.

His mother, though harsh, was a pretty lady. Like him she had light, sandy coloured hair, though hers fell past her shoulders and was curly only at the bottom. Her eyes were blue too, but they didn't have the orange flecks in them that Kaylm's did and so they were without the same rich finish.

"What the hell is wrong with you!?" Victoria demanded. "You bumbling idiot! We're giving you yet another bloody chance to stand up for what's right!"

"Sorry mother…" Kaylm repeated quietly, hoping simply to appease her, for he always tried not to listen too hard to their words.

He didn't really care much for any of them.

"Your mother doesn't need your pathetic apologies!!" His father, Stephen, suddenly erupted, rising from the table like a great ogre.

Kaylm's father had much darker hair than his and fierce, murky brown eyes that were penetrating and relentless. He was a tall, broad man, with the strength of at least two weaker men. Kaylm's older brother, Malcolm, who was already nineteen, was following their father in that trait. With dark hair and piercing eyes of his own he was broad enough and strong enough to be reckoned with already.

Undoubtedly Kaylm too would follow suit, but he was merely sixteen. So, as of yet, he had not broadened like his brother.

Only time and patience would see to altering that.

"Your mother needs to hear you speak bloody sense boy!!" Their father continued, his hands balling into fists on the table and his voice rising to a crescendo.

The string of curses that followed from their father's tongue turned the air darker blue than usual. Kaylm cringed away from the sound whilst Malcolm revelled in it. He was becoming more and more like their father every day, and Stephen encouraged it gladly.

"The final hunt for the demon starts today!!" Stephen went on, spitting the words across the table. "We're going to find it! And we're going to kill it! And that bloody witch too!"

Kaylm felt his blood boil and seethe and he so desperately wanted to bite back, to lash out and silence them.

But before Kaylm even had chance to breathe Stephen became suddenly outraged by his son's insolence. He lifted his balled fist from the table and hammered it into Kaylm's lowered, unprotected head.

His youngest son didn't even see it coming, let alone have chance to defend himself.

He was thrown to the floor in a frenzy.

In an instant both his father and his older brother were upon him, raining blows down at him relentlessly, shouting and bellowing the whole while.

His mother, Victoria, still jabbing and sniping at him, cheered them on, hoping their blows would knock some sense into her useless son.

"She's a witch!!" Kaylm's father roared as he threw punch after punch at his youngest son, desperately trying to cover his face on the hard, stone floor.

"They all were!!" Malcolm joined in, throwing kicks and punches of his own at his younger brother. "No wonder her father was always sick! It was the evil spirits!"

"Why do you think they didn't have any sons!?" Victoria joined in. "They were breeding witches!!"

"Okay!!" Kaylm cried desperately, writhing on the floor trying frantically to get away. "Okay!! OKAY!! I'LL GO!!"

In an instant the beatings ceased and he gasped desperately for breath, clutching at his ribs and his face and back and legs; there wasn't anywhere they had missed.

"Say it!!" Kaylm's father roared, standing over him still.

"I'll go!!" His youngest son urged again.

But it wasn't enough.

Victoria tutted and shook her head in disgust.

Stephen grabbed his son by the scruff of the neck. Lifting him from the ground he struck him square in the face yet again. Kaylm's head flew back and Stephen dropped him heavily to the cold, stone floor.

Malcolm smiled down evilly at his helpless younger brother.

"Say she's a witch!!" Kaylm's father ordered, unrelenting, raising his bloodied fist, once again ready to strike.

"I'll go!" Kaylm repeated, wheezing the words. "She's a witch! I'll go on the hunt!"

Stephen hit him again, even harder again this time and Kaylm's vision blurred terribly.

"Say it again!" His father hissed through cruel, bared teeth.

Kaylm could hardly focus as the room blurred and spun around him. His head pounded and throbbed and he could taste the blood streaming from his nose.

"She's a witch…" He eventually managed to stammer, though he had to force the words from his tongue.

"There, that wasn't so hard, was it sweetheart?" His mother, Victoria, asked then. Her smile was sickly sweet as she spoke and she fingered the loose curls hanging at the bottom of her hair negligently.

Kaylm couldn't find the breath nor the strength to reply.

Without another word, though his father did grunt with slight satisfaction, the three of them sat back down at the table to finish their breakfast.

None of them aided Kaylm, and he didn't ask for it.

He didn't want their help.

Without a word, though with much agony, Kaylm crawled slowly to the stairs and dragged himself up them, one difficult step at a time. He had agreed with them, but that had simply been to escape a beating that may well have killed him.

Silently, he still absolutely refused to yield.

Commencing that afternoon, if he could even walk, he would join the hunt for Marcii and Reaper. He supposed there was no better way he could escape from here to find her. Tyran's men had been combing every inch of the wilderness ever since Marcii had fled.

He reasoned that, now he'd been recruited for the hunt, his best chance of saving Marcii was to find her while Tyran's troops were fighting the demon. Hopefully it would take them long enough to kill it for the two of them to slip away.

It was a ropey plan, he admitted to himself, with plenty of pitfalls. But, considering the circumstances, it was the best he had.

Hauling himself up the last of the steps and into the bathroom, Kaylm gritted his teeth as he splashed cold water on his face, cleaning himself up the best he could.

If Tyran's men did not kill the demon Reaper, he would have to find a way to do it himself, for he absolutely had to save Marcii.

And then together they would leave, never again to return.

Chapter Thirteen

Strangely enough, considering everything that had happened of late, Marcii hadn't had a single dream, nor, perhaps more surprisingly, a nightmare. Not one she could remember anyway.

She woke up feeling drained and tired. At first she thought it was just because she'd gone from sleeping through the night to sleeping through the day and her body was having a hard time adjusting.

But as the weeks went on and her body grew accustomed to Reaper's routine, the young Dougherty did not awake any less exhausted.

Each night when they ventured out under the cover of darkness, Marcii discovered more and more the blissful and undisturbed silence of the night.

She had lived her entire life in a busy, bustling market town, never really knowing peace.

Though she knew virtually nothing of Reaper's past, his life now revolved around such things. He revelled in the tranquillity of silence and stillness like no one she had ever known.

Of course, she knew that's not what other people saw when they laid eyes upon him, for he was a fearsome looking creature.

But he was no beast.

Regardless though, in such matters the truth is often of no consequence.

Just because he was not a monster did not mean he wouldn't be treated as one.

Marcii's strange visions grew more frequent and more vivid as they days went on, though she still had no idea what they were or what was causing them.

She saw all manner of sights that made her blood run ever colder. From widespread rallies and speeches to public floggings and executions, by the time Marcii had witnessed only a meagre handful of the visions delivered upon her, the young Dougherty's sheer will and resolution to oust Tyran from his rule was unmatched.

Many times she tried to convince herself that they were in fact only dreams, and once or twice she even half succeeded in doing so.

But somehow, instinctively, she knew they were much more than that.

She simply could not ignore them, for she knew almost beyond a shadow of a doubt that they were the cold, hard truth.

She felt as if they were important, and that she should heed them, but she had no idea how or why.

If they did have real meaning, as she feared, she knew things in Newmarket were worse than ever.

The thought made her skin crawl and deepened the pit in her stomach, for imagination always trumps knowledge and her mind whispered to her constantly that there was only worse to come.

Chapter Fourteen

Marcii lay awake listening to the sounds of the birds and the trees and even the very cave itself, for the world seemed much more alive during the day than it did at night.

Her life with Reaper was one lived in perpetual darkness.

Not that she minded.

She understood the need for it, absolutely.

But even still, as she lay there, listening to the birdsong echo down from above and wishing she could sit amongst the rustling leaves and swaying branches, the young Dougherty sighed deeply, wondering just where in the world it had all gone wrong.

She pondered that thought, considering if indeed it had actually gone wrong.

She was perhaps happier now than she ever had been, in a strange, free sort of way.

Though there was, admittedly, one thing that she desperately yearned for. Or, perhaps more accurately, one person.

Reaper sat watching as Marcii tossed and turned, troubled by her tumbling thoughts. He remained perfectly still as ever, resting his enormous body back against the flat wall of the cave.

He saw everything.

Though he could not tell exactly what Marcii was thinking, he could tell that something was bothering her.

Usually the young girl slept on his lap to keep warm, but that night, or day, whichever way you look at it, she lay restless on the hard floor by the crackling fire.

She had not been her usual self for a few days now, but Reaper didn't know why.

Though she had not mentioned it again, he knew she wanted to leave.

She wanted to go to Ravenhead.

Alas, for the simple reason that she had not again spoken of it, Reaper knew something was holding her back.

Eventually, unable to lie there any longer, Marcii pushed herself wearily to her feet. Their pattern of waking at night and sleeping during the day meant that her body felt as though it was the middle of the night and her limbs were heavy as lead.

Reaper's eyes watched her every move curiously, though he still kept completely motionless, like a vast, black statue of thick fur and tough, leathery hide.

It was quite an ominous sight really. But Marcii had grown accustomed to Reaper's many curiosities over the past weeks and they no longer surprised her so.

"Can I go outside, please?" Marcii suddenly asked.

Her question broke the long held silence so abruptly that it seemed to echo around the cave a hundred and more times before it finally quieted.

Reaper looked at her for a moment through the dancing orange light of the cave, wondering if that was what had been bothering her the whole time.

He had no way to know about her yearning for Kaylm of course.

Lifting his hands slightly to speak, moving for the first time in hours, he warned her that it would be dangerous to go out during the day. But then, in the same movement, his fingers flickering in the crackling light, he assured her that he would not stop her.

Marcii smiled her thanks and skipped over to hug Reaper, wrapping her tiny arms as far as she could around his massive body.

She stepped back to speak again, but Reaper's hands were already dancing more words.

He asked her if she would like some time to herself for a while.

She had not been alone since he had found her in the woods and he knew that humans were strange creatures. Sometimes they wanted only to be around the company of others, and then other times they wanted nothing more than solitude.

"Is that okay?" Marcii asked, though her eyes betrayed her, indicating to Reaper that was indeed what she wanted.

His hands constructed their reply, assuring her that it was. He promised that he would wait right by the entrance to the cave so that if anything happened she need only call and he would be right there.

"Thank you, Reaper." Marcii replied. As she spoke he pushed himself onto all fours and followed her through towards the entrance of the cave.

The ground sloped upwards and arced into the blinding light cascading down from above. Even though they were being filtered down through the thick canopy the sun's rays were dazzling and Marcii shielded her eyes against their strength.

Reaper, of course, did not need to. He looked up ahead entirely unaffected by the brightness. As he had so aptly explained to Marcii before, his eyes did not need light by which to see and so he was relatively indifferent to it.

Taking a seat just inside the cave entrance, ensuring that he still would not be seen, Reaper crouched and sat, assuming the same position he always did.

Marcii on the other hand, filled with sudden exhilaration, crept upwards towards the cold sun.

All traces of her weariness were gone and she looked back to Reaper only once for reassurance, as if she thought what she was doing was wrong.

His motioning hands told her to enjoy herself, though not to stray too far in case Tyran had troops out on the hillside. She nodded eagerly and smiled warmly at the enormous creature who seemed to have so willingly designated himself her protector.

Without another thought Marcii clambered up the slope that led to the forest and disappeared from Reaper's view.

The giant creature did not move.

But, as ever, his mind was busy at work and his perfect senses stayed constantly attuned, monitoring for even the slightest hint of a sound or movement to suggest that Marcii might need him.

Fearsome though he might have looked, he was gentle and kind and caring, as the young girl had so quickly come to learn.

He was most certainly not about to let any harm come to her.

Chapter Fifteen

The air was freezing and bit at Marcii's skin, but rather than making her shiver, it seemed to revitalise her, freeing her from her worries, even if just for a brief time.

As she rose to her feet, glancing around nervously at first, the forest seemed so full of life and colour that she felt as though at any second it might burst at its seams. The sodden black earth beneath her feet and the rough, brown bark of the trees was so contrasted against the brimming, baby blue sky above, dotted with but a few wispy clouds.

It all seemed most unreal.

She could have sworn that from down in the cave below she'd heard the rustling of leaves in the forest's branches and the sound of birdsong as they flitted between nests. But, of course, it was the middle of a harsh winter, and now that she was here among them, Marcii could see that the trees were empty and bare.

That saddened her for a moment, though she tried not to let it bother her too much.

Though she couldn't really think why, she had imagined before she'd ventured up here that she would find lush green meadows and rippling, swaying forests, all bathed in the glorious light of the soft afternoon sun.

There were huge plains and numerous forests in the distance that Marcii could just about see as she peered through the dense woodland all around her.

But they were not lush as she had hoped, nor bathed in as gentle sunlight. It was the very heart of winter after all and Marcii shouldered her disappointment with a large pinch of realism.

She was wishing for things that simply were not possible in this, the harshest season of them all.

Marcii frolicked slowly through the naked, lifeless trees for a time, running her hands across their freezing bark trunks and passing unheard beneath their leafless branches.

Had the forest been more vivid and full of life her view would have been greatly restricted. But as it was she could see in all directions, for the forest, though dense, was bare as winter's frost.

Unfortunately, she realised, though her own view was improved, the barer the forest remained the more easily their cave might be found.

In the far distance she could see mountains already capped with snow that reached up towards the sky, seeming to part the clouds as they towered over the landscape. In another direction she could see yet more woodlands, equally as leafless and with vast plains surrounding them on all sides like extensive patches of dead man's land.

Ambling this way and that in her wanderings Marcii never strayed too far from Reaper's protection, though admittedly it was nice to be out of the cave.

She knew in which direction Newmarket lay, although she could not see it. The thought made her shudder slightly and she turned immediately back to the forest, but she could not escape the feeling that pervaded even the very trees and earth all about and beneath her.

As she turned, even though she had not turned too quickly or too sharply, Marcii's head began once again to spin. Her feet felt all of a sudden lost beneath her body and she stumbled uncontrollably this way and that, dizzy and dazed beyond belief.

She tried to save herself: to catch it and control it before she fell.

But it was not to be.

Once again, as her head spun faster and faster, as if the world was shaking, her vision hazed and blurred and went black.

She could not hear.

She could not see.

She could not shout for Reaper.

Her feet finally went from beneath her and, unable to stop herself any longer, Marcii fell blindly to the floor.

She hit the ground hard and cracked her head against the unforgiving cobblestones.

Laying there for a moment with her eyes closed, realising all at once that her senses had returned to her, along with a throbbing head, Marcii's fingers clawed at the cold, wet road in horror.

All around her she sensed feet scurrying and scampering in every direction, pounding heavily against the stones.

Her heart pounded as she realised all at once she was no longer alone in the forest.

Finally, knowing she had no choice, she opened her eyes, only to immediately see a heavy boot fling forwards, inches from her face.

She gasped, bracing for the impact.

But once again the figure passed straight through her. Her concern eventually faded into a dull ache and she slowly sat up to look around.

She was back in the square in Newmarket.

Swallowing nervously, Marcii glanced round at the hundreds upon thousands of scurrying figures that rushed this way and that. They walked unwittingly straight through her as they went, without even realising she was there.

She took a very deep breath as she pushed herself carefully up off the floor, for she knew she was wanted by every last one of them.

Likely most of them would have finished her themselves, had they known she was stood right there.

Nonetheless, they didn't.

Marcii had no idea how or why she was there. So, with little other option, she began circling through the vast square inquisitively, wondering many different things.

She had been gone more than just a few weeks now and she was curious to see the results of Tyran's reign.

Marcii still wasn't really sure if what her visions showed her was even the truth. Nonetheless, she had found herself coming to trust them for, she reasoned, what else could they be if not the truth?

Much of what she saw was the same. The same stands and stalls had the same keepers, the same brightly coloured tents were pitched here and there and the same people browsed the same places.

But then, at the same time, much of what she saw was very different.

Instead of tools and food and wares many stalls now sold equipment and weapons and armour, either makeshift or expertly crafted, it didn't seem to matter.

Marcii passed at least a hundred and more enforcers as she slipped quite literally through the crowds, each one armed to the teeth.

There was one thing though that chilled Marcii's bones more than anything, and that was the sight of the townsfolk.

Many of them were also now armed and wore expressions that somehow looked infinitely more lethal than their weapons did. Whether they had purchased swords and spears and armour, or whether they had crafted their own, the sight was still unsettling.

Then, all of a sudden, surging forwards like angry, weaponised sheep, the crowds began to flock towards the centre of the square.

Marcii was relieved not to be caught up between them as she had been in the past.

The sensation was unnerving as people ran through her, but although she did not really want to look, she simply had to see what was going on.

She must be here for a reason.

Perhaps this was it.

She walked directly through the crowd, passing through each and every person in her path, one by one, until she emerged out into the centre of the square itself.

But, as she appeared she found herself abruptly almost face to face with Tyran. Her breath caught in her throat, for he was not the only person that the crowds were gathering to see.

"No…" Marcii breathed, though nobody could hear her.

She felt herself go weak at the knees.

She looked on desperately, knowing she could not do a thing about it.

Tyran spread his arms wide, which seemed only to extend his pot belly as his clothes pulled tight about his middle.

He smiled cruelly and flashed his teeth.

He adored executions.

They built morale and courage: serving better than anything to strengthen his following.

And this particular execution was a very special one, for it would signal the beginning of the second Dreadhunt.

Chapter Sixteen

The first two hangings were swift and accompanied by very little ceremony. They were witches, Tyran claimed, naturally, but they were not the main event. They were merely an appetiser, helping to prepare his audience for what was to follow.

Marcii looked in horror upon the face of Tyran's third victim that day, with the first two still swinging and twitching in the background behind him.

"My people! This man!" Tyran roared, gloating evident in his voice. "This man is not a witch!"

Murmurs amongst the crowds stirred for a moment, but Tyran's raised hand silenced them immediately.

"His crime is much worse!" Tyran went on. "He is one of our own! A priest no less!"

His voice rose and fell dramatically, and it was working. His audience was hooked, completely and utterly, on his every breath.

They had never seen a man executed before.

Gold's murder didn't really count.

This promised to be a much greater spectacle.

"He is a priest! And he has betrayed us! Ladies and gentleman, I give you, Alexander Freeman!"

Instantly the cries for blood began and it was all Tyran's enforcers could do to hold back the surging masses and stop them from killing Alexander themselves.

Marcii could only look on in horror.

She had almost hoped that Alexander had been killed by Tyran's enforcers' beatings, when her family had been burned alive.

At least that would have saved him from a public execution.

It had not been the case though, she now realised.

Unfortunately, Marcii knew what was coming next.

But perhaps even more hauntingly, she knew why.

This was all her fault.

Even amidst the deafening, hollow cries of his people, Tyran did not relent. He only riled them further.

Somehow his booming voice carried above the lot of them, silencing their cries and feeding their hunger.

"This priest! Supposedly one of our own! Helped the witch Marcii Dougherty to escape!!"

And with those words the square erupted into chaos. Not even Tyran's booming voice could overpower the uproar that followed that statement.

For once he was forced to wait for the bitter cries to settle.

He waited a long time, Marcii guessed, but she wasn't really paying all that much attention to what Tyran was saying.

She paced over to Alexander and knelt slowly down beside him.

He was already injured and bleeding and his hands were bound behind his back with coarse rope. Clearly Tyran's enforcers were not softening their approach; if anything they was getting harsher.

Perhaps the power was going to their heads too.

But what could Marcii do to stop them?

What could anybody do?

Tyran's speech went on and his people rallied with him and all the while Marcii sat mournfully with Alexander, though he had no way of knowing she was there.

Marcii didn't even know if she was really there.

This couldn't have been a dream, surely.

But then, she had no idea what else it could be.

She didn't even know if it was real.

Suddenly three of Tyran's enforcers surged forward. They seized Alexander by the scruff of his robe and dragged him across to the hanging platform.

"NO!!" Marcii shrieked, but, as ever, her screams went unheard.

She tried to pull them off him but her hands slipped straight through them.

There was nothing she could do but watch on in horror.

The skies above that only moments ago had been clear, clouded over and darkened menacingly, filling the air with black trepidation.

Marcii's body trembled and shook violently and she cried out over and over again, desperate to do something, anything.

But even still, it was no use.

She looked upon Tyran and his people and his enforcers, shuddering at the sight of the evil he was spreading. She went cold at the thought of the change he had brought here with him.

He had turned Marcii's townsfolk against her. Essentially, whether he cared or not, he had laid waste to everyone she had ever known.

Somewhere amidst the crowd, as her eyes swept all around, Marcii saw Midnight again too. Still the old man's black eyes looked heavy and guilt ridden as he watched the executions, though she could not fathom why such things wracked him so.

And then, from seemingly nowhere, right at the front of the screaming, shouting throngs that so eagerly awaited Alexander's death, Vixen appeared.

Marcii caught her gaze for a mere moment and the young orphan in turn caught hers.

She could see her.

Marcii's heart leapt into her mouth.

How was that possible?

But before Marcii could even draw breath to speak, Vixen disappeared into the masses.

Immediately, not wasting a single second, Marcii took up pursuit.

She needed answers.

She had to know what Vixen knew, for clearly it was more than she'd ever let on.

How had the girl been able to see her, when nobody else could?

Marcii raced through the crowds, not bothering to duck or weave in the way Vixen had to. So, by the time the young orphan had burst from the others side, Marcii had very nearly caught up with her.

Marcii heard the hanging platform creak and drop and the crowds cheered on in exultation. She ignored the sound and blocked out the thought. She hadn't wanted to see it anyway.

She'd seen too many executions already for one lifetime.

Chasing after Vixen still, catching her just before the orphan made it into the first alleyway, Marcii grabbed the young girl by the arm.

In a single movement she spun the child round to face her, clasped her shoulders with her hands and looked her dead in the eye.

Marcii's luminous yellow eyes bore into the tawny brown of Vixen's gaze for a moment, before, in an instant, everything went black again.

When she awoke, her head spinning and her stomach churning, Marcii found herself on the freezing cold floor of the bare forest, numb through to the bone.

Reaper immediately appeared, having only just moments ago emerged from the concealment of the cave entrance. He had heard Marcii's furious cries of anguish and denial and rushed to her aid.

His eyes were filled with worry and concern and he straightaway scooped Marcii up into his warm arms, radiating heat that began instantly to thaw her icy body.

She cried for a minute, clutching at Reaper's thick, shaggy fur like her life depended on it.

But her tears did not last long, for they were replaced by a numbness that swelled ceaselessly inside of her, mixed with deep, endless confusion.

"Was it real?" She asked Reaper, looking up through her watery eyes. "Is he dead?"

The look she received however was not one filled with answers, but rather one that presented only more questions. The enormous, gentle creature that was Reaper did not know what had happened, and so he couldn't give Marcii the words she desired.

The answers she so sorely needed.

The clouds above continued to roll in endlessly, filling the sky from corner to corner with a towering blanket of stormy rainclouds, each one brimming and ready to burst. There came next the ominous roll of thunder. It seemed not to begin in any one place, as lightning shattered across the entire sky like a warning beacon, crying out at the sight below.

And my, what a storm it promised to be.

Chapter Seventeen

Many things had changed in Newmarket, as Marcii had witnessed first-hand.

From the people to the wares, it was no longer filled merely with bustle of commerce, but there was instead an altogether new business that seemed to be taking precedence.

It had become the sole focus of so many of Newmarket's inhabitants that it was as if they were all beginning to think with one mind, and that mind didn't belong to them.

Almost all thought rested exclusively upon the hunt.

It was as if it consumed them.

The market town had become a garrison and in every home the people were mobilising, arming and readying themselves for combat.

Families acquired weapons and armour from the many sellers that Tyran paraded through the town, calling on his contacts from far and wide down in the south.

He made a small fortune on the sales of their wares, naturally, taking a generous cut of all their profits.

It was as if they were preparing for war.

In fact, it seemed the war had already begun.

The demand for steel that Tyran had created trumped all other trade that came through Newmarket. When it arrived, swift and steady, it took over completely. Merchants appeared in droves at

Tyran's command, bringing all of their wares with them from far and wide.

So, when the crowds surged forward to revel in the executions, the steel merchants found themselves, delightedly, amidst a vast throng of hunters all baying for blood.

Kaylm was thrown this way and that as the crowds barged forwards, crushed between them as Marcii had once been.

Nonetheless, he was kept most firmly planted between his father and his older brother, for though he had told them he would join the hunt, they were certainly not about to lengthen his leash.

His face was black and blue and his whole body hurt from the beating he had taken that morning. His ribs heaved painfully with every breath and he struggled to see through his swollen eyes.

That was just as well though, for the dreaded executions were swift to follow, and Kaylm had no desire whatsoever to watch them. He had no choice but to listen to Tyran's speech however, so it came as no surprise when the crowds cheered at the sight of Alexander Freeman's death.

Tyran's speech had his people riled and raring for battle, but it didn't stop with Alexander's hanging and his cruel words continued on relentlessly.

"This demon!" He pressed on, roaring his words even as Alexander's feet still twitched and jerked. "Whatever foul beast it might be! We cannot let it take any more innocent lives!"

The crowds cheered and roared, holding their weapons in the air.

Tyran gestured exuberantly to Alexander's limp, dangling body.

"We may punish those who serve it!" He went on. "But we will never be safe until we have slayed the monster itself!" His voice rose to a bellowing crescendo and his people's blind adoration followed suit.

As if on command, Tyran's enforcers began handing out weapons to anybody who did not yet already have one, children included, passing them swords and axes and clubs of all shapes and sizes.

Then, from somewhere amidst the crowd, the man with the scar that ran around his right eye appeared at Tyran's side. He raised his hands eagerly, encouraging the hordes into yet an even greater frenzy.

Kaylm looked on in disgust.

He didn't even know the man's name, but he recognised him as the one who had reported back to Tyran after they'd first found the demon, the night Marcii had fled.

Kaylm's heart sank at the mere thought.

"HAIL LORD TYRAN!" The man with the scar bellowed, evermore exulting their cruel leader and the crowds screamed their approval.

Kaylm felt physically sick.

He couldn't stand much more of this.

And yet, inevitably, it went on.

Regaling the masses with his undoubtedly wildly embellished escapades, since leading Tyran's men to come face to face with Reaper in the forest the man with the scar had risen to become Tyran's right hand man.

It was he who was to lead their party in the hunt for Reaper.

He vowed to them there and then that together they would vanquish the demon protecting the witch.

They would bring them both to justice.

There was a serious ring of finality to his words, Kaylm thought. The word justice sounded very much like a quick beheading. He doubted they would even bother to bring her back to Newmarket; not all of her at least.

They might bring her head.

"The witch has been using her evil powers to hide from us!" Tyran claimed then, speaking as if he had been out at night amongst the hunting parties.

He hadn't, of course.

A king does not leave his castle when there is no need.

"But she cannot hide with that foul beast forever!" He went on and the crowds roared their agreement.

Surrounding him so that he could not escape, Kaylm's family cheered and screamed with bloodthirsty approval, matched only by the cries of those all around them.

"Tonight we will finish this!" Tyran commanded. "Tonight we will find the demon! We will find the witch! And we will strike them down!"

He rallied the people ready for battle and the bloodlust in their eyes and in their screams chilled Kaylm to his very core.

"If we don't, more evil spirits will arise! If we don't stop her, the witch Marcii Dougherty will continue to haunt us! And we will be the next ones to suffer the same fate as Ravenhead!"

His crowd's cries turned to boos and hisses of defiance at the mention of the abandoned town.

"Newmarket will become a desolate, doomed, plagued wasteland!" Tyran pressed on.

Kaylm disagreed in solitary silence, staring on at the man before them with cold, dead eyes.

He refused to believe it.

Ravenhead was not as he spoke of it.

It was a place for new beginnings.

A place where he and Marcii could start over.

Ravenhead was his only hope.

But his unvoiced dreams were overshadowed by the roaring chant that echoed all around him, reverberating deafeningly in his ears.

No longer did the people of Newmarket quest solely for Marcii's blood, but they wanted Reaper's too.

They needed it, and their murderous words said just as much.

"HUNT THE BEAST!! HUNT THE BEAST!!" They cried. "KILL REAPER!! KILL REAPER!!"

The heavens swelled and clouds crowded above, darkening threateningly, but that only set the tone for their march evermore suitably.

The man with the scar led Tyran's troops to battle once more, only this time with thousands rather than hundreds at his back.

Their chants continued as darkness began to descend slowly upon the day, shrouding and masking it in shadow.

"HUNT THE BEAST!! KILL REAPER!!"

The old man Midnight watched the procession with eyes as coal black as ever. The look he wore was one that fitted him so perfectly, for he had worn it every night now for more decades than he cared to remember.

The guilt painted across his bearded face was always the same, except that of late he had donned it much more often than just when he stared up at the moon.

He leaned heavily on his cane and from between the deep lines all across his face his bottomless black eyes followed the people of Newmarket as they made for the hunt. He watched them go without a sound, though his heart was heavy with dread.

Dragging his scuffed leather shoes as if they weighed a tonne, the deaf, dumb old man turned his back on their parade and left them to it.

He wanted no further part in this.

He felt guilty enough as it was.

Marching through the narrow streets in vast columns, Tyran's troops set immediately to work, holding their torches and their weapons high, drawing strength and bravery from their numbers.

The man with the scar led them out into the wilderness and patrolled his army through the vast hills and valleys and across the great plains. They swept through every forest and every gulley that they came across, heading always in the direction that he had seen the demon, on the night the witch had fled.

It was a thankless task, but he chose to focus their search right at the very spot where Reaper had first revealed himself amidst the trees.

He fanned his troops out in an orderly rabble that was nothing short of a shambles. But, with numbers on their side, they swept through the trees quickly and moved onto the next with great speed.

They might have been looking for a needle in a haystack, but that haystack was growing ever smaller.

Eventually, after several more hours, unable to hold back any longer, the heavens opened and the rains came, triggered by something that none of them understood.

It did not deter them however and the Dreadhunt went on long into the night.

They would not stop until they found the demon.

They would not rest until it was slain and the witch Marcii lay dead by its side.

The people had been poisoned with bitter hatred that wasn't even their own.

And yet the night was still fresh: young as new dawn.

There was still time for worlds to change, if that was to be their fate.

Chapter Eighteen

The thunderstorm raged on, ceasing not even slightly as lighting bolted and clapped across the black, veiled sky.

Echoing endlessly through Reaper's cave and bouncing off the walls in every direction, the sound battered Marcii's ears like a terrifying, godly drumbeat. She shuddered and flinched from the sound as if it would harm her.

Reaper sat opposite her in the darkness, unmoving and silent, seemingly unaffected by the relentless noise all around.

Marcii knew however that something was bothering him.

Though he had not said so, Marcii could tell that he had sensed something was dreadfully wrong. He had told her that they would not hunt that night and that they must not light a fire, for it would be too bright amidst the dark of the storm.

Reaper had never worried so much about that before, Marcii thought.

But then, on that night, even she could tell that something was very different.

Marcii climbed to her feet and crept through the darkness over towards Reaper. Had she not spent the many weeks of late hunting with him at night she would never have been able to even see him in the dark of the cave. But over time her eyes had adjusted to the blackness and become more accustomed to its ways.

They were still not as good as Reaper's she imagined, and undoubtedly they never would be.

Nonetheless, they were better. When Marcii reached him she climbed atop his enormous lap and curled up comfortably amidst his radiating warmth, recoiling from the cold stone of the damp cave all around her.

Marcii's strange visions had terrified her, but when she'd told Reaper of them, he seemed even more afraid than she felt, though of course, he had not shown it.

Marcii knew him well enough by now to know that he did not show his fear in such a way. But equally, it was obvious in many other ways. Marcii had not spoken of it however, for she felt too gripped by the hand of dread to raise it amidst her flurrying thoughts.

They sat together in the darkness and the night wore slowly on, surrounded by the storm and gripped by terror.

Somehow they both knew what was undoubtedly coming, and that no matter what they did it was inevitable.

At some point, through her worry and her fear, Marcii had slipped into a dreamless, fitful slumber. The comforting heat from Reaper's body had quelled her to sleep.

As ever, he remained entirely motionless.

When she eventually roused, it was not Reaper that woke her.

Instead, it was a subtle change in the sound of the storm that stirred Marcii into wakefulness. The lighting still burst across the sky in great streaking flurries and the thunder still growled and rumbled and roared, blanketing the land below fearfully.

That wasn't it though.

There was another sound amidst the darkness and the storm that had awakened Marcii. As she glanced up at Reaper's face, though he had not moved, his ever limitless expressions spoke volumes of what she'd heard, for clearly he had sensed it too.

"What was that?" She whispered fearfully through the darkness of the damp cave, her voice quivering slightly, overpowered by the immense sound of the storm.

Reaper still heard her nonetheless and looked down upon Marcii caringly, though he could not hide the concern spread so evidently across his face.

He made no movement to speak, but Marcii could see quite clearly what he wanted to say. The enormous, terrifying, caring creature that was Reaper lifted her gently to stand, placing her softly on her feet and then rising to all fours himself, stooping under the ceiling of the cave.

His one hand lifted from the floor and made a small, brief signal in the darkness, telling Marcii to wait where she was.

Almost even before Marcii had nodded in response Reaper was heading towards the mouth of the cave. The storm beyond lashed harshly all around, biting at the cave entrance and threatening all who drew near, human and demon alike.

Taking a few steps across the cave so as to keep Reaper in view, Marcii watched him disappear outside into the storm, so heavy and barraging. It swallowed his vast frame effortlessly and Marcii was reminded in that instant exactly how at the mercy of Mother Nature they all were.

After a few minutes, though to the young Dougherty it felt like a lifetime, Reaper finally returned.

His face was sombre and his eyes were heavy and serious, as if he'd just confirmed all his deepest fears. Before his hand had even lifted to speak Marcii already knew what he would say. She threw herself to clutch at Reaper's fur, holding herself close to him and shaking a little.

"What are we going to do?" She asked.

Her words quaked on her precarious breath.

She knew what the sound was that had awoken her, for by now she could hear it clearly between the cracks and rumbles of the thunder.

It was a low, resounding chant that echoed menacingly through the dark of the night, chilling and resounding against the sound of the storm in the darkness.

Reaper had no answer at first, but even so, Marcii knew they had only two choices.

They could either stay in the cave and hope they weren't found.

Or they could leave now and try to escape, but risk facing an army on the Dreadhunt.

Either way, they had to make their decision now, for the sounds of the chants were growing ever closer, as Tyran's troops closed in around them.

Drawing a shuddering breath, Marcii looked up to Reaper and his hands spun into motion.

The young Dougherty swallowed hard and nodded, understanding exactly what Reaper was saying.

The night they were about to face would undoubtedly be fraught with peril.

Chapter Nineteen

Reaper's cave was well hidden and in the dark of the night it was nearly impossible to see. However, with so many troops fanning through the wilderness, driven by such hatred and longing for blood and retribution, it would have perhaps been more unlikely for them to miss it.

The forest was dense with trees looming their thick silhouettes in the night, making the search difficult for Tyran's troops. But his people were driven and in the dead of winter plant life between the thick trunks was sparse.

Tyran's people were committed to finding and destroying the demon and the witch that had been plaguing their town so dreadfully.

There was to be no rest until their evil ways had been put to an end, no matter how much the forest hindered them. Combing every last inch of woodland and field and ravine for miles around, their search was beyond thorough.

Leading them, just as he had promised, was the man with the scar that ran around his right eye.

He did not stop. He did not eat. He did not sleep.

He was truly relentless.

Unfortunately for Marcii and Reaper, his tenacity paid off in the end, as it eventually always will.

He stumbled upon gold, in one form or another.

As he slipped around the ominous silhouette of a thick trunk, keeping his weary eyes peeled, something caught him off guard. His foot suddenly disappeared beneath him and slipped down a trench that he had not at first seen, for it was nearly invisible in the darkness.

He caught his breath as he fell, making hardly a sound and clutching at the tree behind him so as not to fall all the way down.

"What happened!?" A voice hissed from his right, but he waved them off frantically with one hand, silently telling them to keep their mouth shut.

The owner of the voice rushed over, but, rather obediently, did not make another sound. He pulled the man with the scar to his feet and in mere seconds it seemed the entire troop was aware that they'd found something. Scurrying shadows closed in from every direction, drawn to the find.

Fear chilled the air but they felt security in numbers.

The man with the scar kept them silent, striking a few harshly across the face who dared open their mouths.

He could not afford for them to give anything else away.

Surely, if the demon was here, it would already know they had found it.

Soon enough the sloping trench that looked like the entrance to a cave was surrounded by men and women wielding pitchforks and swords and axes, all eagerly awaiting their next instruction.

All signs of fatigue faded away and their angry senses heightened, ready to satisfy the bloodlust that had been building inside of them.

It seemed at long last the time had finally come.

Inside the cave, naturally, Reaper had of course sensed their approach. He could hear them rallying outside the cave entrance and gathering the courage to swarm inside.

He indicated to Marcii with only his expression that Tyran's army had found the cave. She shuddered with dread and swallowed nervously, making not a sound in the darkness.

It seemed their decision to stay put and try to ride out the night had not paid off. They'd taken their chances, hoping their cave would have remained unfound, and now they were trapped.

Marcii looked up at Reaper's looming silhouette in the near pitch black.

An idea formed between them that was perhaps their only chance of escape.

Reaper's vision was unparalleled, or at least as far as Marcii knew. Regardless, he could see all that Tyran's men could not.

"Is there another way out?" Marcii breathed through the darkness, praying that Reaper had a plan.

But when he looked down at her, even though she could barely make out his expression, she knew it didn't hold the miraculous answers she desired.

The first echoing footsteps sounded in Marcii's ears, closer and more terrifying than even the raging storm.

They were inside.

There was no time.

"Reaper!" Marcii hissed, the sound of it filled with horror.

He scooped her immediately up into his arms and silenced her.

Stooping down low, holding himself up on his legs alone, Reaper edged forward and back and forward and back, his mind brimming with indecision.

Marcii shuddered and Reaper felt her fear all too keenly.

He knew there was nothing for it, no matter how much he didn't want to believe it.

The blinding sight of the approaching army's torches flooded unwelcome, orange, dancing light into his home.

There was only one way out now.

Marcii whimpered involuntarily in fear and Reaper pulled her closer to his chest, concealing her within his protective embrace as a parent protects a child.

And indeed he would continue to protect her, for as long as his enormous, demonic body drew breath.

Chapter Twenty

Swords and spears and arrows screamed through the air, whistling squealing echoes through the wide cave. Those shots that missed their target glanced off the stone walls and the ceiling and the floor, sparking as they struck against hard, impenetrable rock.

Not all missed, however.

Those that struck true threatened to bury deep into their huge, shifting target as the great demon surged menacingly forward.

Tyran's men cried out in fear and anger and victory as they swarmed into the cave and attacked. Their burning torches lighted their treacherous path by flickering light. The orange glow revealed the enormous, looming demon heaving towards them from the hidden depths of its lair.

Had he been able to, Reaper would have roared and bellowed as Tyran's army bore down upon him from the cave entrance. They barraged him with pitchforks and axes and all manner of weapons.

But his hide was thick and tough. He did nothing to resist their flurrying strikes. He couldn't, for his arms remained wound protectively around Marcii, encompassing her completely.

Fortunately, the mere mortal weapons of Tyran's men glanced off his body uselessly. All their efforts proved to be futile, for Reaper's hide was too thick to be so easily breached and he was too committed to saving Marcii to back away.

The monstrous demon pushed forward, refusing to yield. His advance forced Tyran's army back in sheer terror, for indeed, by the dancing orange light of their torches he was a dreadful fiend drawn straight from the depths of hell.

Once again, had Reaper been able to roar, he surely would have done, for it would undoubtedly have hastened his advance.

Marcii clung to him with her eyes squeezed tightly shut, gasping for her every breath as she listened to the sounds of shouting anger and screaming blades.

He came so close to the cave entrance, pushing Tyran's army practically all the way up and out into the dense forest above, that he truly thought he would escape without serious injury.

The odd blade had caught a ruffle in his hide here and there, drawing a few touches of blood, but for the most part he was unharmed.

Sadly, it was not to last.

Thrown from his feet by Reaper's relentless advance, the man with the scar spat angrily at the demon.

He refused to yield. He would not be forced to clamber back out into the forest after they had come so far.

Instead, standing his ground firmly, he faced Reaper head on.

He had come too far to back down now and he absolutely refused to be defeated.

As a last resort, having already lost his sword to the demon's seemingly impenetrable hide, the man with the scar lunged forward from the floor and drove his flaming torch into Reaper's massive thigh.

Once again, had he been able to, Reaper would surely have roared in agony. Buckling down to one knee, faltering, the flames swallowed his thick fur and ignited tenfold, scalding his skin beneath his hide.

"THE FIRE!!" The man with the scar roared triumphantly, bounding to his feet.

Tyran's men looked on with renewed vigour.

"USE THE FIRE!!" He bellowed.

Immediately his followers set to work. Those who had scrabbled out into the forest leapt back down into the cave and barraged the demon with their flaming torches.

Reaper writhed this way and that, forced back by their relentless attacks. He cringed as the flames scorched his skin and sent hot steam billowing in all directions.

It was all that the poor monster could do to protect Marcii from the hungry flames. But the more he fought to protect her the more he burned, and the closer she came to suffering too, for his defences faltered more and more by the moment.

Soon he was on his knees, cradling Marcii's body even still within his own, though his protection was growing weaker and weaker.

Every now and then, here and there, a chink in his armour became exposed, revealing Marcii to their attackers.

Her breath caught in her throat every time she saw them.

They looked so fierce, so angry.

How could they possibly hate her so much?

The third time Reaper's arm dropped however, as he wavered more heavily than before, Marcii's gaze fell upon only one person in the crowd of brutes baying for their blood. It was to her truly the only face that stood out from the rest.

Kaylm was black and blue and his eyes were terribly swollen. He stood amongst the throngs as they cheered and bellowed all around him, but he himself did not make a sound.

He was the only one without a look of sheer malice upon his face. Instead, his battered expression was fraught only with worry.

As he caught Marcii's gaze his stricken eyes filled her heart with sorrow.

It lasted for but the briefest of moments however, for in an instant, filling the gap where Reaper's arm had been only seconds ago, a bright, flaring, scalding torch thrust forward.

It blocked Marcii's view and scorched her shoulder terribly.

She screamed as it burned her.

When Reaper heard Marcii's cry of pain, as the flames finally cut through his defences and scalded her bare, flawless skin, the poor, loving demon exploded with fury.

He burst from his recoiling defence and roared with the might of an eruption, shaking the very walls surrounding them and deafening the army at his feet.

The cave itself shuddered at the terrifying sound and Reaper surged forward dreadfully, steaming from every burning limb as he cast his enemies from his path.

Tyran's men were thrown this way and that like puppets as Reaper pummelled through them, casting them off against the walls and the ceiling with his powerful, sweeping steps.

His legs carried him forward with terrifying momentum, though he was hunched over even still.

Torches seared his body as he ran through Tyran's army, but their steaming attacks were made more out of desperation than anything else, as the huge creature parted them like a volatile ocean of steel.

Reaper erupted from the mouth of the cave and out into the dense forest, throwing feeble men in every direction as he did so. Covering Marcii even still, his enormous arms cradled her gently as he glanced round at the scattered army, slowly picking itself up off the floor.

There were men in the forest in every direction for as far as he could see.

Without a moment to waste, knowing that at any second they would be upon him again, Reaper took off at a dead run through the trees.

Branches splintered in every direction as he ran and men continued to fly through the air in his wake.

He careered left and right and only just missed the thick tree trunks in his haste. Once even, unable to turn in time, he battered head on into a tree and smashed through it as if it were made from mere paper.

He felled the huge oak without even breaking his stride, sending it soaring up into the air and then tumbling down with a terrifying, crashing sound like thunder that carried for miles all around.

Tyran's army immediately took up pursuit, hunting both Reaper and Marcii down relentlessly through the thick forest.

They hoped that the trees blocking the demon's path and the wounds that they had inflicted would slow the foul brute enough for them to catch it.

Through the pounding rain they hunted the pair.

They were so close they could practically taste the witch's blood, and that of her demon.

Soon they would have them both.

Chapter Twenty-One

The rain grew thicker and heavier, thrashing Reaper as he cascaded through the dense trees, limping more and more with every step.

Though Marcii knew his pain was worsening, for she could feel him juddering as he ran, Reaper would not relent. He charged faster and faster, almost even blindly through the driving rain battering down through the thin canopy above.

"Reaper!" Marcii called, her voice barely reaching out from the protective cocoon he still had her sealed within. "Reaper please!" She urged.

Eventually, gradually, his huge chest heaving, Reaper slowed to a walk, but he did not stop.

He would not.

He glanced over his shoulder, fearing the worst.

But, for now at least, they seemed to be alone.

"Are you okay?" Marcii whispered, afraid to raise her voice too loud.

She ran her hand gently over one of Reaper's burns and felt him cringe.

"Sorry." She apologised, feeling foolish.

Her own shoulder seared agony through her skin; she couldn't imagine the pain Reaper must be in.

She had to help him if she could.

"Let me down." Marcii urged. "Let me look at your burns."

But Reaper refused. Glancing down, he told her with his eyes that Tyran's men were still close. There was too much danger for them to stop now.

Suddenly a voice cut through the darkness and startled them both.

It wasn't entirely clear, but it sounded like it was calling Marcii's name.

Reaper whipped round like lighting, crouching low, peering all around, ready to fight or flee again in an instant.

The voice didn't sound again at first and even as Reaper surveyed the trees with his impossibly perfect eyes Marcii could feel how tense his enormous body was.

Seconds turned into what felt like hours in the edgy night.

When the voice eventually called out again, this time much closer, Marcii almost jumped out of her skin.

"Marcii." It called. "Up here."

Reaper jumped back and Marcii gasped in both fear and surprise, looking up as the enormous demon pulled her to safety.

For a moment her eyes searched the darkness, glancing between the bare branches in the poor light. Reaper, of course, saw immediately what it took Marcii several seconds to find.

Vixen.

"What the…?" Marcii started, but she struggled to finish.

What in the world was Vixen doing here?

All of a sudden Reaper seemed to relax, rising slowly from his crouched stance to look at Vixen more closely.

The young orphan girl sat up the high branches of a bare tree in the darkness, higher even than Reaper was tall. She dropped down a few feet and took a seat upon the thickest section of a lower branch, descending to Reaper's head height.

The massive creature that even still held Marcii rose to his full height, levelling his gaze with that of the young orphan girl, and stared her straight in the eye.

For a moment Vixen said not another word.

She just stared back into Reaper's deep, jet black eyes like coal, lost in them amidst the darkness all around.

And then, all of a sudden, Reaper smiled. The tension in his body faded and melted away as if he knew something about the strange young girl that Marcii did not.

She seemed somehow to fill him with a calm and reassured confidence.

Vixen reached out slowly and ran her hand gently down the tough, leathery hide of Reaper's cheek.

The more that Marcii looked on, seeing clearly that something was passing between the young orphan and the monstrous demon, the less she understood what it was.

"What are you doing here?" Marcii hissed, breaking the silence of the bare forest. The trees were filled with intruders that swarmed between its vast trunks, searching for their victims, and all the while they were just stood around upon the whims of a little girl.

Vixen raised her hand in the darkness to silence Marcii and Reaper looked down briefly at her with an expression that insisted she complied.

Marcii hushed her noise, though her unanswered question still hung in the air. As far as she could see there was no obvious or logical reply. Nonetheless, Vixen waited even still, listening to the sounds of the night, and Marcii remained utterly dumbfounded.

Then the sounds of scraping steel and banging iron carried through the dense, dark forest, reaching Marcii's ears and filling her once more with dread.

Though they too listened intently, and probably heard much more than the young Dougherty did, Vixen and Reaper seemed not to be affected so by the chilling sounds. It was as if there was a fourth person amongst them, whispering quietly in their ears, calming them, yet ignoring Marcii altogether.

Or at least, as far as she could tell, she felt like she was being ignored.

"Wait here a minute." Vixen instructed them suddenly, glancing around briefly through the driving rainfall, still having not answered Marcii's question. "There's a group approaching." She explained. "Don't move. They will pass."

The young orphan sounded so certain, as if she'd seen this all pass before and was simply remembering what would happen next.

Marcii's eyes grew wider by the moment, though Reaper seemed unfazed and even relaxed in Vixen's bizarre presence.

But then, Marcii supposed, Reaper was rather unique himself. She reasoned somehow that she probably shouldn't have been so surprised.

"There's a ravine, there." Vixen continued, indicating with her tiny hand through the darkness of the forest.

Marcii and Reaper looked on, following her gaze. Reaper nodded confidently and Marcii could sense he knew exactly what she spoke of.

"Pass through the ravine and go west." The young orphan instructed. "They won't be able to follow you."

Marcii wondered how in the world Vixen knew these things, as she stared on incredulously through the darkness, straining her eyes to see what Reaper undoubtedly saw.

Reaper raised his hand to Vixen's height, holding Marcii still with his other arm, and thanked Vixen with a small, almost indiscernible gesture.

Suddenly the sound of voices cut through the trees, frighteningly close.

Reaper crouched down low and clutched Marcii tightly to his chest.

He still didn't seem tense, even though every hair on Marcii's body stood on end in fear.

But sure enough, just as Vixen had said, though the patrol drew close, close enough even for Marcii to see their looming silhouettes from between the trees, they did not find them.

Their voices were hushed and harsh but they carried a great distance through the night, as voices always will. They spoke only of finding the witch and her demon and slitting both their throats.

Marcii's blood ran cold and her breaths grew shallow. If it had not been for Reaper holding her so close, her fear would likely have consumed her.

She couldn't believe Tyran had instilled such hatred in his people.

She was no witch.

And Reaper was no demon.

Was he?

Soon the silhouettes vanished into the night and Reaper rose to his full height once more.

Marcii looked back up to the branch upon which Vixen had sat, only to find that she was no longer there.

At least she was growing accustomed to some things, it seemed. The young orphan's disappearance no longer shocked her so. She still didn't understand it, but she had at least expected it, sooner or later.

Now that the danger had mostly passed, they hoped, Marcii dropped to the floor and she and Reaper made their way together through the still pouring rain towards the elusive ravine that Vixen had spoken of.

Her legs felt heavy as she forced one foot in front of the other. The soggy ground gave way unhelpfully beneath her feet and served only to tire her further.

She could feel the damp cold through her leather shoes and she kept close at Reaper's side for his warmth.

Soon the ground beneath Marcii's feet turned from marsh to rocks and they found themselves clambering over great boulders. Eventually Marcii saw that they were sliding between the steep sides of a great ravine that cut impossibly out of the ground on either side of her.

Marcii wondered what Vixen had meant when she'd told them Tyran's men would not have been able to follow them, but she didn't have to wait long for her answer.

All of a sudden Reaper's hands darted out to stop Marcii in her tracks. She looked up inquisitively through the hammering rain at the enormous creature.

"What is it?" She asked, confused.

Reaper indicated with his hand to the steep, rocky walls that rose up around them, and then pointed to the floor before them.

Marcii was confused, for all she could see in the darkness were rocks and grass and mud.

But when Reaper took a pace forwards and his massive leg like a tree trunk sank at least a foot into the ground, Marcii realised all of a sudden why they would not be followed.

The rain was running off the sides of the rocky ravine in great torrents, creating a deadly marsh all the way through.

Without a sound or even a gesture Reaper scooped Marcii once again up into his arms and lifted her to sit upon one of his enormous shoulders. Without wasting another moment, the vast creature strode immediately into the bog, sinking deeper and deeper with every step he took.

His powerful strides forced their way through the thick slush, parting it either side of his massive legs with a disgusting gloopy sound that made Marcii's skin crawl.

In his wake Reaper left the ground in a state of churned turmoil, as the mud grew ever deeper, to the point even where Reaper was up to above his waist in it.

Had he not been so tall, or so powerful, he would certainly either have gotten stuck or drowned in the muck.

Voices echoed behind them in the darkness, but Marcii felt safer than she had done all night. Not only did she still have Reaper protecting her, but there was a virtually impassable bog between them and Tyran's men.

The further Reaper waded, pressing on relentlessly through the thick, slimy water, the quieter the voices became. The rewarding silence all around engulfed them completely, disturbed only by the sound of Reaper's struggling steps as he carried the young Marcii Dougherty to safety.

Chapter Twenty-Two

Marcii had never seen Reaper struggle so. Even though they'd made it back onto flat, solid ground, his head hung lower and lower with every step. But it wasn't crossing through the ravine that had taken its toll on Reaper, Marcii suddenly realised, coming all at once to her senses.

Marcii halted and Reaper followed suit, wondering what the matter was.

"Stop, Reaper." The young Dougherty insisted. "Let me look at your wounds."

With a small gesture of his hands Reaper insisted that he was fine, but Marcii was not about to take no for an answer and she stubbornly refused to let the enormous creature defy her wishes.

"Reaper!" She replied firmly. "You're injured! Let me look!"

Finally conceding to Marcii's words, seeing that she was not about to relent, Reaper obediently dropped to one knee, knowing that she was deadly serious.

Just as she had feared, upon closer inspection, Marcii found that Reaper's burns and cuts were not as mild as he was making out. He was still bleeding where Tyran's men had here and there managed to pierce his thick hide and from their torches his skin was scalded terribly.

"Oh Reaper…" Marcii breathed, running her hands gently around his wounds, examining his arms and chest and back and legs.

Suddenly Reaper's hands burst into life, knowing that Marcii was concerned for him. He explained to her that his injuries were not fatal, but if they weren't sealed, they would take a long time to heal.

"What can I do?" Marcii asked, wanting of course to help.

Reaper's hands continued to dance, though she could see him wince slightly every time he moved. He instructed her to gather handfuls of mud from the drenched ground and cover his burns and cuts.

"Mud?" Marcii questioned, eyeing his cuts with concern. "Won't they get infected?" She would never have put mud on her own wounds, surely. And with that mere thought, her own burned shoulder seemed to sear into life once again.

They needed water to clean them.

But Reaper's hands wove yet more intricate and delicate patterns in the air. Undoubtedly his gestures were far too complex to understand, but Marcii knew exactly what he was telling her.

He explained that the dirt would not infect his wounds like it might for humans. He told Marcii that just as his skin was thicker than hers, so too was his blood. The mud would harden and help seal his wounds and stop the bleeding. Then, in time, it would peel and flake off, leaving him fully healed.

Marcii on the other hand, though the wound on her shoulder was not as serious as Reaper's injuries, still needed to find fresh water.

Taking his word for gospel, wincing slightly as she scooped handfuls of mud from the soggy ground, Marcii applied it liberally all over Reaper's wounds. He groaned inwardly as she smeared the dirt over his cuts and burns, but he endured in motionless silence.

After a few minutes she had lathered all of his injuries in mud and Reaper stood once again to his feet and rose to full height.

His hands flickered a swift sign, thanking Marcii for her care.

She smiled warmly through the night.

"You're welcome." She replied. "Which way?" She asked him then.

His hands spun into motion once more. He told her they would keep going west, towards Ravenhead. He assured her that there was a stream not too far away that would be full after all the rainfall. They could use that to treat her shoulder.

There was much more Reaper would have liked to have done for her wound, but there were simply not the resources available.

As Reaper's hands spoke Marcii couldn't help but notice a deep regret and sorrow that coursed through him, probably without him even realising.

"How do you know which way is west?" Marcii asked, for there were no stars by which to see.

Marcii didn't know that Reaper's anguish was due to finally relenting and heading for Ravenhead, for he gave nothing of it away.

She simply presumed it was from his wounds.

It was on Vixen's word that he would lead Marcii there, and he was certainly not about to go back on what She'd asked of him.

Reaper's hands wove patterns then that Marcii had not seen from him before, and though she understood what he was telling her, it didn't quite make sense.

"The ground tells you?" Marcii questioned, confused. "I thought people navigated by the stars?"

Her err however had not been in her understanding of his words, but indeed in her own thoughts.

Reaper's hands danced again, explaining to her that indeed people did navigate using the stars, but that such things were done out of necessity, rather than choice.

She had misunderstood his meaning. It wasn't the ground that helped him, he explained, but the very earth itself. The world was alive: the trees, the wind, the rain. He could feel it with his every breath and it guided him like nothing else.

Marcii looked on, astonished.

Reaper continued, revealing pure truths that surely only he could understand.

His hands danced for the young Dougherty and she marvelled at them, as he explained to her that most humans would never be able to feel the world in the way that he did.

In the same way as they used the stars to navigate their own planet, so far away and disconnected, they would always look afar beyond their own reach to understand what was right in front of their eyes. No matter how hard they looked, because of that mere fact, they would never find all that they wished to know.

They were too cut off from their own world, from their home. So much so that they simply could not comprehend it.

They never would.

A cavity opened in Marcii's chest where surely her heart had once been.

If this was what it meant to be human, for now she saw more clearly than she ever had done, she didn't want to be.

She would have been better off a demon.

Regardless of what the world thought of her, Reaper cared for her always.

Surely, no matter what he was, he was infinitely better than all the evil Tyran had instilled.

It seemed that to be demonic was kinder and infinitely less cruel than to be human for even a second.

For a brief time that night, amidst the darkness all around, Marcii longed to be free from her human self. She yearned to feel the same connection to the world that Reaper did.

For a moment at least, without a second thought, she longed to be a demon.

Chapter Twenty-Three

The rest of the night passed quickly. Even before sunrise approached on the distant horizon Marcii was exhausted. As ever, Reaper seemed not to be tired, but clearly his wounds had taken their toll upon him. He seemed relieved when they eventually found shelter to stop and rest.

The stream he'd told Marcii of had indeed been close, allowing her to thoroughly clean her burn and see, thankfully, that it wasn't as bad as it felt. The patch on her shoulder that the licking flames had caught felt tight and hot. It would heal quickly though, for she was young and had every reason to.

Morning soon came and brought sunrise along with it. Though they weren't fortunate enough to locate a cave, Marcii and Reaper sought shelter amidst the thickest copse of trees they could find.

It shielded them from the exposing sunlight and retained at least a little of Reaper's vast warmth, for every time she stopped moving Marcii's muscles threatened to seize up in the relentless cold.

Certainly without Reaper she would have succumbed to its icy clutches a long time ago.

Marcii slept heavily in drowning exhaustion, not waking even once.

Reaper did not sleep, but his body was in dire need of rest. As he sat, unmoving as ever, with Marcii curled up on his lap, his mind raced while his body recovered.

His demonic thoughts tumbled and churned, filled with dreadful memories that swam in bottomless regret.

Marcii knew not of Reaper's torment, or at least he hoped she had not sensed as such.

She didn't need to know.

He didn't want her to know.

Not yet at least.

Marcii didn't yet know what Vixen was either.

Reaper hadn't known of her before admittedly, but he'd sensed it as soon as he'd seen the young orphan.

Like he'd told Marcii, he could sense things that most humans could not.

Things that Marcii could not feel.

Or, at the very least, things she could not yet feel.

Darkness rolled around again as the world turned laboriously on, casting its endless shadows over the forests and plains and ravines. The night stirred Marcii and Reaper into motion once more as it spun.

Fortune was at last favouring them it seemed, for they met no one in the new blackness and made very good time.

Marcii knew from the many tales she'd heard that it took three full days to reach Ravenhead from Newmarket.

It took her and Reaper much less time however, partly they were already partway there, and then also because the enormous demon carried Marcii some of the way too. Reaper was much recuperated and he was eager to put as much distance between them and Tyran's men as possible.

Marcii felt more alive and more free than she had done in a very long time. It was not that she'd felt trapped in Reaper's cave, but instead now that Newmarket was fading into a distant memory, she could finally let its grasp on her loose, even if only slightly.

The sky above was clear for a change, with not a cloud in sight. The ground was still damp underfoot and the drenched fields that stretched out before them seemed to reflect the brilliant light of the moon. It's misty white glow was encompassed all around by twinkling, boundless stars, painted across the pitch black canvas sky in their millions.

Reaper turned to Marcii in the moonlight and wove a dance with his enormous hands, clear as day in the glorious whiteness.

He assured her that they were very nearly halfway to Ravenhead and that they would reach the abandoned town the following night.

"How do you know?" Marcii asked.

Clearly she still had no idea exactly how well Reaper knew this route, and indeed Ravenhead itself. She simply presumed that it was just another of Reaper's extraordinary demonic talents.

Nonetheless, though Reaper could quite clearly see how unaware Marcii still remained, he knew now was still not the time to reveal what he knew. And, not only that, but he also very much doubted that he should be the one to divulge to Marcii all that she would eventually need to know.

Reaper's hands wove his reply as they walked, speaking only the truth and answering Marcii's question fully, but at the same time, revealing almost nothing.

He explained to her that he could sense a deep gorge up ahead, dropping almost a hundred metres down through rock and stone, carved through the earth over time by a rushing, racing river that coursed along its bottom.

He told her that the gorge cut across the land from north to south, blocking their path, and there were only one or two safe places to cross. Purely by chance, the gorge marked the exact halfway point between Newmarket and Ravenhead.

Reaper told Marcii that, when she saw it, she would see deep into the world in a way that most people couldn't even dream of.

There was perhaps much more to his words than Reaper let on, but the young Dougherty didn't quite pick up on it.

The enormous demon was not deterred however.

Reaper suspected that in time she would come to understand.

The rich, moist grasslands gave way to a rough, rocky carpet underfoot as they approached the deep gully.

He slowed his pace in the dim light and instructed Marcii to do the same. Though he could see the perilous edge as clear as day, it came up fast in the darkness, and he most certainly did not want his young Dougherty stumbling upon it all of a sudden.

"Is this it?" Marcii asked, her voice catching for some reason as her body filled with excited apprehension.

There was no need for Reaper to answer her though, for as she spoke his enormous right hand reached out to hold her back. Even with eyes that were nowhere near as sharp as Reaper's, Marcii could see the black abyss that opened up in the ground before them. It cut across the land like a deep scar left behind by a blade that surely could be wielded only by a God.

It looked to be about two dozen feet across, more in some places and less in others.

If she listened hard enough Marcii could hear the faint roaring of the crashing waters below, far down in the canyon: the very waters that had so abruptly and unexpectedly carved the gorge through this landscape.

Marcii felt suddenly filled with questions that brimmed and overflowed her body, tiny next to Reaper's.

"What's it doing here?" She asked of him.

Reaper looked at her for a moment, wondering whether perhaps he'd been wrong.

Already she was more perceptive than she probably even knew.

"I mean, when everything else is fields and forests, why all this rock right in the middle?" Marcii asked again, rewording her question, thinking Reaper hadn't answered because her question hadn't made sense.

The great creature at her side smiled kindly and lifted his hands to speak, understanding her intrigue wholly, and with great respect in fact, for curiosity is always a mark to take note of.

He told her that the river and the rocks were here long before the fields and the forests, so, if anything, it was they who were out of place, for they had intruded upon the gorge, not the other way around.

"Intruded?" Marcii queried. "You make it sound like they're human…"

But Reaper's hands quickly corrected her mistake. He assured Marcii that they were not human at all, but instead much, much more.

"More?" She questioned and his huge hands wove their fluid agreement right before her eyes.

He explained that the rocks and the fields and the forests had been here long before humans and that they would likely be here long after too. His thick fingers wove a hundred and more intricate signs and shapes and Marcii swallowed them hungrily with her eyes, for yet again they spoke of truths she had never even dreamed of.

Reaper told her that many years and decades and centuries might seem like a long time for a man. But for Mother Nature a century passes by in a mere heartbeat, as her home continues to turn endlessly. Many millennia would slip by and very little would change, for when you are talking about altering an entire world, it takes much longer than a mere thousand years.

Marcii couldn't quite believe what Reaper was telling her, but at the same time, there was no way she could ever doubt him.

Man had been here very little time at all, he told her. And likely it wouldn't be long before they were gone again too.

"Gone!?" Marcii asked, a little startled, and even concerned.

Reaper only smiled and cast his hands into yet more words, telling her not to worry. People had been here more than a few thousand years already, he assured her; they would likely remain for at least a little while longer.

"It just sounds like we're all so insignificant..." Marcii noted, her voice laced with sorrow.

Reaper thought for a moment before he replied, choosing his words carefully.

Eventually his hands spun into motion once again.

He agreed with her at first, telling her that anything would seem insignificant if you always looked at it in that way.

"I suppose that's true..." Marcii conceded, though she was not convinced.

Nonetheless, Reaper's hands wove their magic once again and revealed a truth to Marcii that perhaps she had absolutely no right to know.

But then, on the other hand, she had possibly the only right.

He revealed to the young Dougherty then that Mother Nature did not, and would not, interfere with the workings of man.

She has no interest in human quarrels, for they are often petty and always pointless.

Marcii nodded in sombre agreement, though she did not speak, for she had seen the consequences of such quarrels first hand.

But Reaper continued, pressing on. He told Marcii that sometimes, if the need arose, and more importantly if they were willing to listen, Mother Nature would speak to a chosen few.

He explained that She was not heartless and cruel as many believed, but instead kind and nurturing. When those who lived in her world cared for their home, She too would care for them, just as any mother should.

Chapter Twenty-Four

The canyon widened and narrowed alternately. Marcii could see quite clearly here and there, even amidst the clear darkness, where massive chunks of rock had broken away from the impossibly steep walls of the gorge and plummeted down into the river below.

At no point did the walls of the canyon weave close enough together for Marcii to cross.

Nonetheless, Reaper led her to the very edge of the deathly precipice, looking to do exactly that.

"Reaper…" Marcii started, her voice wavering.

The enormous creature that was Reaper turned to the young Dougherty and his hands stirred into sudden flurries of motion.

He explained that they would have to go for more than a few miles either way to reach a point where she could cross without him, and that it would slow them down considerably.

"Okay…" Marcii replied nervously. She understood the logic to his words, but that wasn't to say they didn't fill her with fear and apprehension.

He asked her if she was ready.

At first Marcii didn't reply.

Reaper only smiled, understanding her hesitation.

His hands spun into speech yet again, reassuring Marcii that he had her, and that as long as he lived he would not let any harm come to her.

"Okay." Marcii repeated, with much more certainty now. She knew there was nothing but truth in Reaper's words and they filled her with confidence anew.

As he held out his massive arm Marcii clambered up into Reaper's warm embrace. She clutched at his thick fur and hide and he held her close and safe.

With his free hand he asked if she was ready.

Marcii found she could only nod and swallowed hard, shouldering her fear as best she could.

Stepping slowly to the edge of the canyon, facing off directly against the vicious scar that cut so deeply across the landscape, Reaper squared his enormous stance and judged the distance in the darkness with his perfect vision.

Squatting down and tensing his powerful legs like huge springs, Reaper readied himself.

He seemed to pause for only a mere moment and Marcii held her breath tightly, clenching her hands into tight, balled fists around Reaper's warm, matted fur.

In an instant, released like a coiled spring, Reaper exploded from the ground and launched himself and Marcii into the air.

They sailed over the vast emptiness of the canyon in a blur of motion.

The cold wind rushed into Marcii's face with the speed of Reaper's jump, stealing her breath away and robbing her for a moment of the ability to regain it.

Her heart leapt into her mouth, mirroring Reaper's action in of itself, and they careered through the perfect black sky and towards the opposite side of the steep, jagged ravine.

The arcing leap seemed to last a lifetime, but in reality it was only mere seconds before the ground came rushing up on them once again.

Reaper had judged the distance perfectly. Just as they began to descend horrifyingly towards the river far below, solid ground once again appeared beneath them.

He smashed into the floor with a crack so loud that it echoed for miles all around, making the very earth shudder beneath him. Having chosen his spot carefully, there was no danger of any part of the cliff face breaking away.

As he hammered into the ground, cradling Marcii gently in his arms, he dropped to one knee to help absorb the impact and cupped her head tenderly in one massive hand, ensuring she did not get whiplash.

He knew the workings of the human body well, as he had already demonstrated to Marcii several times. He knew he would have to protect his young Dougherty; her frame was just as fragile as they all were, if not more so.

Catching her breath as Reaper rose slowly to his feet, Marcii looked up in something of a windswept daze.

As he lowered her slowly and carefully to the ground the young girl took her weight on slightly wobbly legs.

With one hand Reaper asked if she was okay.

"Oh my life…" Came her somewhat unsteady reply, though it was followed by a nervous laugh that told him she was perfectly fine.

Reaper smiled comfortingly.

Marcii was indeed strong, more so than most of mankind it seemed.

He knew in that moment she would cope with anything and everything she needed to.

Well, almost anything.

For the rest of that night they continued their journey, making good time through the early morning as dawn fast approached.

Marcii walked some of the way and Reaper carried her the rest: it was much faster that way and they covered much more ground.

Just as before, when the sun finally reared its head upon the horizon, Reaper found them a suitable place to rest and recuperate for the day. That gave Marcii a chance to sleep and allowed their wounds to fully heal.

Though Reaper's injuries had been more severe than hers, his body healed faster than Marcii's ever would. By the time evening came round once more, though his wounds had been deep and malicious, the enormous creature Reaper was fully recovered.

It was just before dawn the following morning when they at last reached their destination.

Marcii's heart and stomach were so filled with nervous excitement as they approached Ravenhead that she felt as if an army of butterflies was dancing through her body.

She had dreamed of this moment ever since she and Kaylm had first spoken of running away. As she thought of her dear friend a sharp pang of regret struck at her chest.

The memory of him outside of Reaper's cave stuck in Marcii's mind, battered and bruised. Memories of him taunted her terribly and she knew that those images would likely haunt her forevermore.

Reaper was filled with dismay all of his own.

Although he was troubled by memories altogether different to Marcii's, they were at the same time so hauntingly similar they may as well have been one and the same.

Needless to say, Reaper's enormous body brimmed with dread.

As the odd pair approached the abandoned settlement, each tormented, ironically, by their own demons, Ravenhead loomed out of the darkness before them, undisturbed for so many years gone by.

But, as had been the case many a time of late, that was all about to change.

Chapter Twenty-Five

The mood of the men was mixed as they returned to Newmarket.

Some were furious that the evil witch and her beastly demon had escaped their grasp, whilst others had not expected to find the devilish monstrosity in the first place. Those amongst them were simply grateful to be alive.

Speaking of which, surely only by way of a miracle, not a single life had been lost during the hunt.

Even though they had found and indeed truly fought both the beast and its creator, they had all returned home with their lives, with but a few meagre injuries between them.

Luck and good fortune had clearly been with them.

But then, of course, when they were fighting to rid the world of such foul and evil beings, how could it not?

The man with the scar surveyed Tyran's troops as they re-entered the outskirts of Newmarket.

Undoubtedly Lord Tyran would not be best pleased, and though he would never have admitted it, the man with the scar feared for his life upon their return. Their Lord was always quick to anger and his arm was long and wrathful.

Tyran's men appeared before their Lord, dishevelled and demotivated. But more to the point, empty handed.

He surveyed them with piercing eyes as they filed dutifully and almost mournfully into the square in the centre of Newmarket.

He could tell in a heartbeat by the looks on their faces that they'd found the witch Marcii Dougherty, and at the same time that they'd allowed her to escape.

The evil tyrant was not the only one to scrutinise the return of his men however. There were plenty of others who hadn't joined the hunt who all looked on just as curiously.

They saw no real injuries, and though of course they could not account for every man in a single glance, it seemed to be the case that all had returned.

There was one man however, looking on with eyes as black as coal, whom had not joined the hunt, on account of being deaf and dumb and riddled with old age.

Though his other senses might have betrayed him, his pitch black eyes were as keen as ever.

The old man Midnight saw every face that reappeared in the square and the fearful expressions cast across them. He saw awe mixed with terror, and certainty mixed with doubt. Haunted eyed glanced about nervously.

Those amongst them who had once been certain that the witch Marcii's demon would undoubtedly slay them all, now held themselves with obvious doubt. They had returned and were surrounded still by their fellow townsfolk, alive and almost entirely unharmed no less.

Nevertheless, such minor doubt, especially at this stage, would never have been enough to shake Tyran's irrefutable hold, and his people's hesitation simmered just below their unwavering, fearful obedience.

Midnight saw immediately that one face was missing amongst the crowd and no matter how hard he looked, and looked, and looked again, he only saw the mother, father and brother.

The young boy Kaylm Evans, for some reason, was not amongst them.

When Tyran's words rang out across the square, reverberating endlessly down every alleyway and street, his tone was sharp and displeased.

Without even waiting for an explanation his berating tongue lashed out across the crowds, slicing through the air at them from every direction.

He expressed, at quite some length, his extensive displeasure, and was most certainly not ungenerous with his far reaching vocabulary.

Perhaps luck and good fortune were indeed with the troops, for now it was undoubtedly only by the stroke of an absolute miracle that none of them found themselves attached to the end of a very short rope.

Threats were made, as they were bound to be, but orders were given in equal measure.

Tyran made it very clear that failure was not acceptable. He announced that he would lead the next hunt himself, save having to endure their incompetence once again.

A rather light sentence for the men, all things considered.

They dispersed back to their homes in droves, seeking their beds in exhausted relief.

The man himself, Lord Tyran, did not find rest so easily however. He seethed and simmered for hours upon their failure.

Stupid!

How could he have been so foolish as to let them go alone!?

And where was the cretin witch Marcii Dougherty now!?

There was no way of knowing.

He did know one thing for certain at least.

He knew he would not make the same mistake again.

Next time, he would lead the Dreadhunt himself.

Chapter Twenty-Six

Kaylm found himself alone in the dark of the night.

All around him he heard the wind and the rain pelting down, barraging him endlessly as he stumbled blindly through the forest.

He had lost the rest of Tyran's troop, quite purposefully. It hadn't been difficult. After they'd found Marcii in the cave with the demon, utter chaos had ensued.

Even though he now found himself alone in a strange and dangerous place, threatened by hypothermia and undoubtedly any number of forest dwelling creatures, Kaylm feared only for Marcii's life.

He had to find her before any of the others did.

The demon had her.

He had to get to her before it killed her.

Though, the more he thought on it, the more he couldn't help but remember how the demon seemed to have been protecting her.

Surely if it had wanted her dead, it would have already killed her? Or just left her to die at the hands of Tyran's men?

He didn't know.

Young Master Evans wasn't really sure of anything anymore.

All he did know was that Marcii was out there somewhere, and he would not stop until he found her.

He continued on through the forest, hoping desperately that he would stumble across some sign of her, or the demon.

Anything.

But it seemed the monster was too experienced in evasion, or Kaylm was too inexperienced in tracking. Either way, after hours of searching and mindless wandering, Kaylm had found only exhaustion.

His exhaustion and fatigue turned, as they usually will, into frustration, which itself manifested into hopelessness and despair.

Such things are often an endless, inescapable cycle.

In his desperation Kaylm didn't notice the figure watching him from afar, off between the trees in the darkness. As he tripped and stumbled on the looming shadow in the distance kept pace with him effortlessly. It made no effort to remain unseen or unheard; Kaylm was simply too weary to pick up on it.

As he continued on, tripping over protruding roots and misplaced rocks, the silhouette mirrored his every step perfectly, marking time in the darkness.

At last, after many missed opportunities, as is often the way, Kaylm finally noticed a flicker of movement out of the corner of his eye.

His head snapped over his right shoulder and his eyes shot across the dense, bare forest. Scanning the trees, his gaze settled immediately upon the figure that had been following him, for still it made no attempt to hide.

As he looked upon it for a moment it froze perfectly still.

"What the…?" Kaylm breathed into the night, trying to make out the ghostly outline in the darkness. "Marcii…?"

Fleeting shards of hope raced through Kaylm's bloodstream and he surged forward with vigour anew. But even as he started towards the figure it slipped in and out of sight between the trees, moving swiftly away from him.

The faster he ran, the faster the figure moved, and soon Kaylm found his tired legs practically sprinting through the trees, carrying him as fast as they possibly could.

He wasn't sure how long he was chasing after the strange silhouette for, hoping desperately that it was Marcii, but it was long enough for his heavy legs to be burning and his cold lungs to be heaving.

The shape ahead of him shifted and moulded through the forest like it belonged there, perhaps even more so than the trees themselves. The very idea of that seemed impossible to Kaylm, but it happened anyway.

Eventually, just as his body was about to give up, the figure slipped between two trees and vanished from sight.

"Wait!" Kaylm cried out breathlessly, but there was only air enough in his drained lungs for that single syllable.

He followed the silhouette as far as he could, but once it disappeared from view he had nothing left to go on. All of a sudden Kaylm found himself face to face with nothing but a steep sided ravine. The tall walls of the gully were harsh and rocky and the rainwater ran off them in great torrents, feeding into the base on the ravine and turning it into a deep, boggy marsh.

The peaty ground was churned and mashed almost beyond recognition, even as more and more water poured in. It took Kaylm a little while to discern what he was actually looking at.

Footprints.

Waterlogged and pulverised admittedly, but footprints nonetheless.

Enormous footprints.

"Marcii..." Kaylm whispered to himself again, gazing yearningly through the ravine in the darkness.

He could see quite clearly the tracks left behind by the monster Reaper, even in the darkness, as they crossed straight through the impassable bog and off into the distance.

"West..." Kaylm gasped, sudden realisation flooding through his exhausted body. "Ravenhead..."

Vixen watched from some ways off between the trees as the young boy Kaylm Evans made his insights and revelations. She had led him this far, but that was all she was able to do. He would have to make the journey without her.

He was certainly determined enough; she could see that quite clearly.

In just the same way as she had done for Marcii, several times now, Vixen remained the figure concealed in the background. She was the silhouette hidden amongst the shadows, and there was much more to her than could ever possibly meet the eye.

Chapter Twenty-Seven

Ravenhead was a ghostly place.

At first glance it seemed stripped bare of all life and shape and form: a mere shell of its former self.

But the more that Marcii and Reaper explored, passing through the abandoned streets with their shadows pressing upon the cold, grey stone, the more the young Dougherty came to realise exactly what this place was.

Though there was no sight or sound of even a single soul, not yet anyway, Marcii couldn't help but feel like she was passing through a deathly silent home. But as the hairs on the back of her neck stood on end, equally she couldn't help but feel a soul's presence, still resonating in this eerie, abandoned ruin.

It was a mining village, or it had been at one time.

Now left desolate, the hundreds upon hundreds of rows of tiny stone houses had vines and grass and trees growing in them, twisting through every crack and bursting from every weakness they found within the stone. Some buildings clung as best they could to all that remained of their slate, tiled roofs, whilst others had lost the battle long ago. Those that hadn't managed to remain standing were left exposed. Inside and out they were unprotected against every aspect of the harsh and ever changing elements that engulfed the land.

Where there had once been roads the ground had in many cases been committed back to nature. In some places they had survived, but in others the cobblestones had been split and cracked into great shards as Mother Nature had claimed back what was rightfully Hers.

"I've wanted to come here for years…" Marcii admitted suddenly, breaking the silence that had clung to them.

She and Reaper had paced without a sound through the forsaken streets so cautiously that the echo of her voice seemed to shatter the very air itself.

Reaper did not reply.

Instead, in the dark of the very early morning, only an hour or so before sunrise, memories that he had long since tried and failed to forget came flooding back to him in droves.

But, as ever, he did not speak on them, and Marcii did not pick up on his unspoken suffering.

"When things were bad…" She went on. "I used to think if I ran away, if Kaylm and I ran away, we could come here. We could start a new life. We could forget everything about Newmarket. I could forget my family; he could forget his. We could just be happy…"

Her words continued to echo through the dark streets and reverberated off in every direction as if they didn't belong anywhere.

It was the first time in her life, aside from her and Kaylm's brief, fleeting, desperate conversations about running away, that Marcii had actually ever admitted just how badly she'd always wanted to leave Newmarket.

Reaper listened to her words, hollowed over the years by unhappiness, and more recently by fear too.

To a certain extent he understood Marcii's painful longings, but perhaps from the opposite end of the scale.

His earliest memories were of Ravenhead, and of his family.

This was his home.

He had never wanted to abandon this place.

But, just as quickly as he'd arrived here, he'd been forced to leave, by powers completely beyond his control.

And then, even after that, yet more pain had Reaper been forced to endure, for his family were soon stripped from him, leaving him all alone in the world.

The colossal creature looked down at Marcii Dougherty then through the dark of the very early morning with a strange mixture of emotions painted across his beastly face.

In more ways than she could possibly imagine, though it was by no fault of her own, it was Marcii who was responsible for Reaper's loneliness.

But there was no way she could have known that.

Not yet anyhow.

She didn't even know what he was, let alone why he was.

But Reaper was not bitter; not in the slightest.

If he had been, he would not have saved her from Tyran's men in the forest, when he'd found her half frozen to death.

He would have just let her die.

"I used to hear stories about this place…" Marcii recalled, her voice interrupting Reaper's thoughts, though probably for the better.

He looked away again and surveyed the ruins around them. Although this was his home, he had never seen the place thriving with life. He had only ever witnessed the desertion.

He'd seen it right from the very beginning, when the townsfolk had all first fled.

"I've heard lots of stories…" Marcii went on. "But I don't think anyone really knows why it's abandoned…"

The ironic contrast of Marcii's words against Reaper's thoughts was more than a little painful for the enormous creature, but even still he did not speak on it.

He knew the time would come, but as of yet nothing had changed; it was still no more his place to say than it had been before.

He simply listened as they walked. Marcii told him of all the stories and folktales she'd grown up hearing about this desolated place, however wild they might have seemed.

Reaper tried his best to hide the pain that cut so deeply through him, further and further with every word that Marcii breathed. But the more that she remembered, indeed so too did the enormous creature at her side.

Poor Reaper struggled more and more with every step to conceal his ever growing agony from the young girl.

Her recollected words struck at his heart and became truer and truer by the moment.

Even so, as the morning rolled slowly and agonisingly in, Marcii was unware of Reaper's anguish.

It may not have been entirely her fault, but at least some of his suffering was Marcii's doing.

Surely, without a shadow of a doubt, there was no force in the world that could change all that he'd lost.

Chapter Twenty-Eight

"I remember hearing once that it was an epidemic of some kind…" Marcii recalled, thinking back many hazy years to even the smallest, most fleeting moment that she could recollect. "A plague of some kind…" She went on. "Brought to Ravenhead by rats, I think someone told me once…"

Reaper nodded, listening as Marcii regaled him, telling him of all the things he knew not to be true.

"Someone else told me it's because the mines were too dangerous…" She continued. "One day there was a terrible collapse. It killed hundreds of people, and trapped hundreds more…"

They had not yet reached the entrance to the mines and still wandered the abandoned streets like two stars lost in the endless universe. Marcii glanced about on a whim, looking for the mines with her eyes, though unconsciously searching for something else entirely.

"But then I've always wondered if that's true…" She breathed, distracted, her words trailing off as her eyes eventually settled upon what they sought.

Raven's Keep came into view.

Marcii's eyes widened and Reaper's heart sank.

His hands made not even the slightest motion as his eyes too settled upon the familiar sight.

Remaining silent as ever, he listened to the inaccuracies of all that Marcii had been told of this forsaken place over the years.

That wasn't what had happened at all.

"But what if it was something else...?" Marcii contemplated aloud, though her words trailed off again as her breath faded.

It was as if the shared vision of Raven's Keep had somehow joined their minds for the briefest of moments, and Marcii's wandering thoughts stepped a keystone closer to the truth.

"What if it was something that happened here..." She whispered, her eyes widening. "And not something that came from elsewhere..."

How close to the truth Marcii was growing surprised Reaper somewhat, but then, he supposed he should have suspected it would happen in time, considering what she was.

Marcii's train of thought took another turn then, steering directly towards the tower from which she could not tear her gaze.

"I've heard stories about Raven's Keep too..." She whispered, barely loud enough to hear even her own words.

Reaper, of course, heard her every breath, and hung on each sound just as heavily as the last.

"Kaylm and I wanted to run away and watch the sun set from the top of the tower..." The young Dougherty admitted with a slight chuckle. Her laugh was followed by a weary sigh however, knowing she would likely never see him again, able only to pray that he was still alive.

Reaper remained motionless as they wandered even still, though his chest balled into a tight fist that threatened to suffocate him, for he knew where Marcii's words were leading her.

"I've heard even more stories about Raven than I have about why Ravenhead is abandoned…" She mused aloud.

Reaper grimaced.

"I heard she was the most beautiful woman in all the land…" Marcii breathed, turning at last to Reaper, forcefully tearing her gaze from the tower.

She looked him dead in the eye.

In an instant, more to conceal his anguish than for any other reason, Reaper's hands stirred into motion.

They flickered and danced and Marcii smiled as she watched his words form before her.

He told her that true beauty lies in the eye of the beholder.

"That's true…" Marcii agreed, smiling warmly at the silent, enormous creature beside her, thinking a thousand and more tumbling thoughts.

Reaper's enormous hands dropped back to his sides and Marcii took a deep breath.

"I used to hear stories that when Raven lived here, in her Keep, that people flocked from miles and miles around just to catch a glimpse of her…" Marcii recalled.

She looked up again at the tower, dotted sporadically here and there with a few weathered potholes, but no beautiful young woman.

Marcii looked to Reaper again and once more his hands spun into motion.

He asked if her parents had told her the stories.

The young Dougherty laughed shorty, and rather curtly, though then she looked apologetically up at Reaper.

"No." She replied simply. "My mother didn't care for stories. Once or twice my father tried to tell me a tale or two, but my mother made his life difficult whenever he did."

Reaper asked her why, admittedly a little shocked by Marcii's reaction and response.

"Because she didn't care much for my father either." She replied, shrugging her shoulders a little as if such things were commonplace.

Sadly, it is likely that they are; probably much more so than they should be.

Marcii sighed again.

"I bet Raven wasn't like that…" She mused, and the pain that seared through Reaper in that moment was like none he had experienced for a very long time.

And it just so happened that as she spoke Marcii glanced back up at Reaper and saw upon his face an expression that she had never before witnessed.

Though he gave very little away, it was the first time he had let slip anything at all of how he felt.

It was obvious that the concealed look on his face was one of sorrow and pain and regret.

Marcii saw that the mere mention of Raven's name brought her enormous, demonic friend almost unmatched sorrow.

The young Dougherty realised all of a sudden that there was yet even more to Reaper than she'd first thought, and that in fact he might indeed know what happened in Ravenhead, and why it was abandoned so.

Chapter Twenty-Nine

The demonic creature Reaper rose to his full height as menacingly as he could. His enormous legs rooted into the ground and his massive shoulders and arms flexed threateningly.

Marcii cowered back, afraid.

She had never seen Reaper like this. Even when Tyran's men had invaded his cave he had been unsure.

Clearly something had changed, and it had been so ever since they'd arrived at Ravenhead, only three or four days earlier.

Reaper seemed to be so on edge and filled with angst so deep rooted that it was simply unshakeable.

And now, far in the distance, too far for Marcii to see yet, Reaper had seen somebody, or something, approaching their abandoned haven.

The young Dougherty did not need Reaper to tell her it was someone from Newmarket: one of Tyran's underlings no doubt. She could see by his reaction he was ready to fight, and to the death it seemed.

She couldn't believe how quickly things had gotten to this point.

It was as if Reaper had nothing left to live for. As if, whatever it was from his past that still plagued him, that he'd lost, it had been stolen from him all over again.

The figure in the distance approached steadily and was soon close enough for Marcii to distinguish its shape against the rolling hills and sporadic islands of bark and branches. It was definitely a person, but they weren't yet close enough for her to make out enough detail so that she might recognise who it was.

Reaper had other ideas though, it seemed. He took several long, slow, striding steps forward, warning of his intentions all too clearly. His head was low and his gaze was level, focused, dreadful.

Marcii understood his concern, for she too was filled with apprehension and fear. But, nevertheless, she didn't like seeing this new side to her dear friend.

It was a side of him that she had truly never known existed and it poured fear into her bones and into her heart. Though, it filled her with angst in a completely different way to that of the hated and beloved Tyran.

This was a much rawer, more natural fear, rather than something derived from conspiracy and malice and intimidation.

She supposed there was only one way to think of it.

It was simply the nature of the demonic.

"Reaper…" Marcii started, stepping forward cautiously to the enormous beast drawn up so terrifyingly before her.

He did not reply.

But then, just as Marcii drew breath to speak his name once more, the approaching figure crested the next hill. The young man's gaze settled upon the

monstrous demon and the tiny girl awaiting his arrival
with such apprehension.

When Marcii exhaled, after a moment or so,
for her breath caught tightly in her throat, it was not
Reaper's name that she whispered, but a different one
altogether.

"Kaylm…"

The name hung in the air delicately, as if at
any moment it might be swept away on the faintest
breeze.

She couldn't believe her eyes.

Even Reaper felt the sound cut through his
anger, holding him so fiercely. His shoulders
suddenly relaxed as he realised all at once that there
was no threat to be had here.

Marcii had spoken to him of that name many
times now, and every time she had her voice was
filled with more love and greater adoration and
deeper longing than the last.

Reaper even found that he recognised the boy,
when he looked a little more closely. He had been
amongst the troops who had attempted to kill him.
Only now his young face was not so bruised and
battered.

The great demon could only begin to imagine,
at the hands of his fellow man, how much this poor
soul must have suffered, just for the chance to see
Marcii again.

The enormous creature softened his heart and
turned to look upon his young friend Marcii
Dougherty, outcast so awfully from her own kin.

Her eyes were all too clearly filled with hope
and desire, and Reaper realised in that moment

exactly how much Kaylm meant to her, even if she'd never said it out loud.

He'd felt that kind of love before.

The kind that is so vast it is simply uncontainable.

Love is the only emotion so unexplainable and unique, that not even the greatest of writers could hope to contain it within their meagre words.

There was no way Reaper was going to rob Marcii of the chance to feel such a thing, for he knew how boundless such emotions and passions were.

The poor demon's only hope was that the cost of it would not be too great for Marcii and Kaylm: that being mixed up so deeply in such dreadful events would not come back to haunt them, for there would undoubtedly be dire consequences for their devotion to each other.

Chapter Thirty

"Marcii!" Kaylm exclaimed, overjoyed as she ran out from the ruins to meet him. The young Dougherty fell into his arms and squealed with delight as he swept her up in his tight embrace.

For a brief, blissful moment all of Marcii's reservations about being human melted away and vanished. Her despair disappeared into an abyss so bottomless that she felt nothing but the simple joy and pleasure of connection with Kaylm.

Such a thing can usually only be felt with someone through deep, adjoining emotion, and that is something found all too rarely nowadays.

Reaper remained still, as he often did, and surveyed the sight with his jet black eyes like coal.

He felt both sorrow and happiness all at once.

Though naturally he and Marcii had grown close, their relationship would never be what hers and Kaylm's was.

There was simply no way it could be.

Reaper could sense in an instant that what she and Kaylm shared was unrivalled, and such a thing was beautiful to see.

As he had so recently been reminded, Reaper knew exactly how such a love felt, and so he stayed put, giving them that precious moment and allowing Marcii time to invite Kaylm to meet him.

The enormous creature was a gentle, caring soul; Marcii knew that through and through.

But to look at, quite on the contrary, Reaper was a fearsome, beastly monstrosity, and he knew it.

People had always feared him.

Well, most people at least.

He didn't turn away, but at the same time he remained unseen and unheard. Instead, he turned his eyes filled with blackness towards the endless sky and swallowed its vastness in his demonic gaze.

It was early in the evening and there were still remnants of the day smeared across the purplish expanse above them. Stars had already decided to simmer here and there across the cold cloudless canvas and, although the sunlight was still fading, the moon was already in full view. It cast brilliant white, luminescent light across the masterpiece, refracted undoubtedly through time itself from so unbelievably far away.

Reaper sighed heavily.

As he had explained briefly to Marcii, though admittedly he had barely touched the surface, he felt a connection to this world so strong that it was indescribable. In fact, the only thing he could compare it to was the very connection she and Kaylm shared.

But, at the same time, it was somehow altogether different.

He relied on the connection. He could feel the very earth and ground and rocks and trees pulsating through his body with his every heartbeat, surging through him like the blood that flowed through his veins. When the wind curved around his enormous body it seemed not to brush past him, but to entwine itself between his very limbs, caressing him as it moved.

He found his demonic thoughts wandering as he stared up at the sky, realising that he knew nothing of the worlds that lay beyond his own. Every notion seemed to tumble headlong into the next as he pondered everything and nothing all at once.

Soon enough though his thoughts ran away with him completely and he sighed heavily once again.

The monstrous creature named Reaper supposed that, although it was near impossible to explain, the connection he felt with the world was a part of him. And, in just the same way, the connection that Marcii and Kaylm shared was unbreakable also.

It had probably been so for their entire lives, likely before they'd even known it themselves.

Without one, surely the other would also fall.

Reaper had experienced this himself. As Marcii had so repeatedly, though also unwittingly reminded him of late, he had once too felt such a connection, and to a human no less.

He vowed silently to himself, and to Mother Nature, who had so caringly filled the emptiness that had hollowed out inside of him after his loss, that he would do everything in his power to protect what Marcii and Kaylm shared.

Glancing back over, he saw the two of them approaching. He swallowed all thoughts of himself and focused instead on the young girl Marcii, whose life he had so selflessly saved. He looked upon her companion too. Kaylm had, in turn, so gallantly come looking for her, undoubtedly prepared to face down any demonic threat so as to save her life also.

It seemed that, against all odds, there were many who cared for the young Dougherty in this world, both human and demonic alike.

And then yet also, perhaps there were forces even greater than mere men and demons who pondered upon Marcii's every move.

But enough of such thoughts for now.

The boy looked terrified.

Reaper did his best to ease their first meeting, crouching low to the ground and dropping slowly to sit, assuming the least threatening posture he could possibly manage for a creature of such monstrous dimensions.

"Kaylm..." Marcii began gently, taking the young boy's hand in her own, for his face was white as a sheet. "This is my friend, Reaper..." She told him, as reassuringly as she could possibly manage, considering the circumstances. "He saved my life..."

After a few wary moments, still understandably unsure, Kaylm nodded quickly and nervously. He did not speak, though a little colour did just about manage to return to his cheeks.

Marcii smiled.

"Reaper..." Marcii said then, looking her enormous, demonic friend in his jet black coal eyes.

His expression spoke a thousand and more words, as it always did, and he smiled as warmly as he could manage, though the sight was perhaps not as comforting as he'd intended as his perfectly white teeth flashed in the twilight.

"This is Kaylm..."

Reaper turned his blackened gaze upon the boy Kaylm Evans. He smiled approvingly and slowly raised his hands to his chest.

His fingers wove and danced and flickered into motion, greeting Kaylm and welcoming him to Ravenhead.

The young Evans' eyes widened in disbelief and all colour that had crept back into view upon his face swiftly faded to white once more. He realised all at once that, not only was this monstrous, ape-like creature indeed a friend, but that he could understand it.

Reaper's hands continued to weave and trace invisible lines through the air and Marcii spoke with him at great length. Kaylm saw that the demon understood everything Marcii said, though he only ever replied with his hands, making not a sound.

And every time, somehow each of his realisations filled with more disbelief than the last, Kaylm understood exactly what the dreadful creature was saying too.

But perhaps what was even more incredulous, if that were even possible, was that the more that Reaper spoke, though he made not a sound, the faster Kaylm's fears fell away from him. The terrifying demon reduced his high barriers to rubble, stripping him of his uncertainty, and within minutes he had found his tongue.

In fact, within less than half an hour, as darkness settled more fully over them, the bizarre looking company of three retreated from the cold. They delved deeper into the heart of the abandoned settlement Ravenhead and found shelter from the night.

As they spoke, unveiling all that had happened in such a short space of time on opposite sides of the same tale, Kaylm even found himself coming to like Reaper.

The demon was, to all extents and purposes, friendly. He seemed kind and he was clearly very protective of Marcii: a quality that the two of them certainly shared.

When Kaylm had first spied Ravenhead in the distance both he and Reaper had expected a fight. But now, quite on the contrary, they found themselves actually enjoying each other's company.

It warmed Marcii through to her very core to watch her two closest friends grow into companions so quickly. Quite often throughout the evening she just sat back and watched them talking, occasionally allowing a satisfied, contented smile to creep across her face.

The night wore on and the air grew desperately cold, ensuring that they knew it was most certainly the thick heart of winter. By midnight a layer of sharp frost had settled upon the now not so desolate Ravenhead.

Kaylm did not last far beyond that however, for he was weary and hungry and exhausted from his journey. Reaper hunted briefly, leaving Marcii and Kaylm alone for an hour or so. By the time the enormous creature returned however, carrying the spoils of his endeavour with him, he found the pair of them fast asleep together by the fire.

It was the first night in a long time that Marcii had slept well without curling into Reaper's warm lap.

The sight of Kaylm lay protectively beside Marcii warmed Reaper's demonic heart.

Whistling with a shrill cry, the harsh evening wind cut through the long unused streets of Ravenhead like a ship parts the waves through heavy fog.

Despite the bite of winter however, contentedness lay upon the three of them for at least that brief moment in time.

Whilst frost set about blanketing the land, the young Dougherty slept soundly in the protective arms of her lost Evans.

As ever, Reaper sat motionless and watchful. He had some inclination of what might follow, for he had seen much of this before.

Although, as is usually always the way, there was still undoubtedly much more to come that he had never before witnessed.

In fact, there was much to come that nobody had ever before seen, regardless of how many times these events had recurred.

Chapter Thirty-One

"They forced me to join the hunt." Kaylm explained to Marcii as they wandered through the empty streets of the mysterious Ravenhead.

"I know." The young Dougherty replied.

Kaylm looked confused for a moment.

"What do you mean?" He asked her, and Marcii realised she now had to somehow explain her strange visions.

"I saw you…" She began, though perhaps not in a way that made it easy for herself to explain. "I saw you in the street, in Newmarket…" She attempted.

"When?" Kaylm asked, confused.

"When the two women with black hair were being taken to the square to be executed. But I wasn't actually there. I was just, watching…" Marcii replied, blarting the whole thing out in one go, reasoning that there was only so much confusion she could instil with a single breath.

"I don't understand…" Kaylm replied, even more confused, naturally.

"It was like I had a vision…" Marcii tried again, attempting to elaborate on her explanation, which had been sketchy at best. "I went all dizzy, my head was spinning, and then the next moment, when I opened my eyes, I was back in Newmarket."

"Right…" Kaylm replied, waiting for more.

"It's happened quite a few times…" Marcii went on. "The first time it happened I saw the two women. You were watching them being dragged to the square, but you wouldn't go with them…"

Kaylm looked shocked, but he said nothing, allowing Marcii to continue.

"So then, when I saw you at the cave, and your face…" She trailed off at that point and her lip quivered slightly at the memory.

"I understand." Kaylm finally intervened. "You saw my face and you knew I'd been forced into it?"

Marcii nodded, taking a deep, shuddering breath as she did so.

"I knew it was my best chance of seeing you again…" He admitted, even a little sheepishly.

Marcii smiled gratefully.

"But how did you know your vision was real?" He asked her then. "I mean, how did you know it wasn't just a dream?"

"I didn't." Marcii admitted. "But it didn't feel like a dream…"

"What about the others?" Kaylm asked. "You said it had happened more than once?"

Suddenly Marcii's eyes widened and Kaylm saw her very soul quiver inside of her.

"Marcii?" He urged. "What is it? What's wrong?"

But she could not speak, for it came flooding back to her all at once. She'd tried so hard to forget it all that she thought she almost had done.

Almost.

"Alexander…" She breathed.

Kaylm's face turned a ghostly white.

"You were there?" He whispered, after a few moments of silence had quivered between them.

Marcii nodded for a moment, but then her tongue took over.

"Well, no…" She interrupted her own reply. "I suppose I wasn't, but I saw what was happening…"

Truly now they both realised that these visions, whatever they were, were indeed most significant. Marcii had spoken of truths to Kaylm that she surely could never have known, and vice versa, he had confirmed for her that Alexander's death had indeed taken place.

Or, perhaps more accurately, his murder.

It had not been simply a figment of her imagination, and that terrible truth threatened to rear up and swallow Marcii whole.

Reaper had not accompanied Kaylm and Marcii, and instead sat alone with his deep, demonic thoughts.

Within the sheltered confines of an old house with no roof, Reaper sat with his back pressed up against the cold, hard, stone wall that was the rear of the building.

In many ways it reminded him of his cave.

It was cramped, yet at the same time spacious. It offered shelter and security, whilst simultaneously being completely open to invasion.

But there was one thing that the roofless house gave Reaper that his cave never could: a window into his past.

It was something that had lived within him always, for Ravenhead was the very place he had come into existence.

His memory of it had never faded and he had never longed to be here any less.

But now that he sat staring up at Raven's Keep, swimming much deeper than just up to his waist in thought, he realised all at once why they'd never returned here.

He had always known it would have hurt her more, so much more, than it could ever hurt him.

Things had changed now though.

She had been taken from him, and he felt both of their pain tenfold.

With endless pity and sorrow in her eyes, a ghostly figure looked down upon Reaper from the very top of the tower, meeting his gaze with long lost recognition.

Her deeply lined faced showed her many years evidently, though she was still a very attractive woman. Her dead straight, jet black hair, streaked here and there with grey, framed her aged features perfectly. With luminescent violet eyes she stared down at the enormous creature Reaper, seeing that he had finally come home.

But the sight of him with his two companions brought nothing but pain afresh into the ghostly woman's heart and soul. For these two he had with him, a young man and woman no less, could never replace the two she had lost.

No matter what happened, or even if Reaper had returned with the intention to stay, it would make no difference.

In her endless grief, she would surely mourn them for all eternity.

All of a sudden, overwhelmed by emotion, as we pitiful beings usually are, Marcii thanked Kaylm elaborately for coming to find her.

She had missed him dearly.

But then, in almost the same breath, she scolded him for deceiving his family, for she couldn't bear the thought of the repercussions he might suffer upon his return to Newmarket.

But then, did he have to go back?

Why should he?

Surely there was no need?

He was Marcii's dearest friend in the whole world, except perhaps for Reaper, though their bond was altogether different.

She simply could not bear the thought of Kaylm leaving her again.

He promised her he would come back, and in turn she begged of him not to go.

Of course though, as ever, he had only her in his thoughts and in his heart. He insisted that he must return to Newmarket, save them sending out a search party to find him. Undoubtedly his absence would have been noted most keenly by his family and yet more tales of conspiracy would be circulating.

The young Evans could not bear the thought of endangering his Marcii: any risk he might take, no matter how great, was better than that.

He told her of how awful things had become in Newmarket and how Tyran's hold over the people was nothing if not absolute.

They spoke again of Alexander Freeman and how the priest, like many others, had suffered so terribly at the hands of Tyran.

Kaylm explained how his wife had found out about his affair. Marcii nodded with agreement, admitting to Kaylm that she had known too, only days before she'd fled.

Naturally, as is often the way with a woman's scorn, especially when she has been betrayed so, she proceeded immediately to consult with her Lord Tyran.

Whether she actually suspected that her husband had helped Marcii escape or not, it mattered not. Her words stung with the same venom and had the desired effect.

Somewhat guiltily, and with something of a bitter irony, Marcii admitted to Kaylm that in fact Alexander had indeed helped her to escape.

But as he undoubtedly always would, forever at her side, Kaylm assured her that none of this was her doing.

Had Alexander not had his affair, he would surely still be alive to this day, whether he'd helped her or not.

Then Kaylm spoke of Marcii's family, though his words were clearly filled with apprehension, for he had no idea whether she'd seen what had happened, either with her own eyes or in a vision.

She told him of all that she'd seen as she'd desperately fled Newmarket. He nodded solemnly as she told him her story, though he barely spoke at all, knowing not the words that were needed.

The day wore on and afternoon was swift to encroach upon them.

Somehow, in the space of just a single night, Marcii had switched completely back into the rhythm of wakeful days and sleep filled nights that she had known for her entire life, up to the point of meeting Reaper.

She hadn't realised quite how much she could miss something as simple as daylight, regardless of how dimly the winter sunshine matched up to that of warm summer afternoons.

The air was bitterly cold and Marcii pulled her thick sheepskin around the both of them as they sat down behind a low wall. The stone was cold but it kept them out of the wind. Marcii regaled Kaylm all the while with tales of how Reaper had saved her and cared for her.

The harsh, lashing winds cut through Ravenhead particularly fiercely for the rest of that day and soon enough they all retreated back inside, into a building that still had a roof, to ride out the worst of the storm that was undoubtedly on the horizon.

But little did they know the severity of what was to come, for all that had happened up to that point, all the good and all the bad, was merely the dawn of something else entirely.

Chapter Thirty-Two

Another night passed and for yet another darkness Marcii slept in Kaylm's arms, across on the opposite side of the fire from which Reaper sat.

The enormous creature gazed down upon the pair of them for many hours as the night shifted slowly by, his eyes cutting through the orange and red and yellow flames that divided them.

All things considered, Reaper had not known Marcii a very long time, but that mattered not. Even in that short period, having spent virtually every moment with her, Reaper had never seen her as happy as she'd been that past day.

When morning eventually rolled laboriously around the sun peeked its head curiously over the horizon far to the east and all the remaining darkness seemed startled by the fresh light.

Motionless even still, Reaper had not budged all night.

When Marcii and Kaylm stirred finally into wakefulness, awoken by the sunlight streaming across their exposed faces, their eyes laid sight first of all upon Reaper. His gaze rested solidly upon the pair of them even still, just as it had done all night long.

The enormous creature lifted his hands up from where they lay in his empty lap and formed his first words of the day, greeting them both a good morning.

"Good morning Reaper." Kaylm replied first. "Happy Dew." He added then, smiling crookedly.

There was a merry, yet slightly mournful tone to his voice and Marcii looked on at him incredulously.

"Is it really that time!?" She exclaimed, shocked at just how long she had been absent from Newmarket.

She hadn't realised she had been gone for that amount of time and couldn't quite believe it.

Poor Reaper had not the faintest idea what they were talking about. He twisted his hands into yet another shape: one that he'd never made before. Though, of course, Marcii and Kaylm understood him in an instant.

"Dew." Marcii confirmed, nodding her head as Reaper gestured to them. "Winter's Dew."

"It's a celebration." Kaylm explained. "They say it comes from a time when there were no markets and people only worked the fields. One winter, when the morning dew that covered the fields froze solid for a full week, the people could not work." He went on. Marcii intervened to continue the story.

"They could only rest for the week." She told Reaper. "It happened like clockwork at the same time every year. It was so regular that by the time a year eventually came where it didn't happen, the people took the week for grace anyway. They'd gotten so used to it that it had become tradition, and it still is to this day."

"Well…" Kaylm cut in, his voice dropping somewhat. "It was…"

"What do you mean!?" Marcii demanded disbelievingly, shocked at the thought that there would be no Dew.

"Tyran announced last week that while the hunt for you is still on there is no time to rest. He insisted that the danger of still having a murderous witch running free is too great."

Marcii's lip practically curled under with hatred and anger.

Somehow, without her even being there, he had made Marcii responsible.

"He's a monster." She breathed menacingly.

"He convinced everyone that if we were to stop the hunt, even for a day, you would seize the chance to strike us down." Kaylm went on.

Marcii cursed foully, throwing her hands up in frustration. Kaylm did the best he could to calm her and quell her surging fury.

"I know, I know." He assured her. "I know it's nonsense. But that's why I have to go back."

Marcii looked at Kaylm through stricken eyes.

He had insisted the same thing only the day before.

"They'll only keep hunting you." He explained again. "They might even be out searching for me, though I doubt it…" He admitted. "If I go back, I can tell them you captured me, but that I escaped, and then I'll send them all searching in the wrong direction. I'll lead them on a wild goose chase."

Marcii's heart jumped at the thought, for Kaylm's plan was fraught with peril.

They might not believe him.

They might torture him.

They might kill him.

He knew all this of course.

But it wasn't himself he was concerned for; Reaper could see that quite evidently.

There was silence for a few minutes as Kaylm's words sunk in and hung heavily all around them.

Eventually, though his words did not break the quiet, Reaper spoke, and his hands danced with the sound of forced merriment.

He wished the young Dougherty and Evans both a happy Winter's Dew. Then, without any hint of an explanation, he rose slowly to his feet, towering over the both of them.

Assuring them that he would be back, Reaper vanished from sight.

He bounded from the house and from the abandoned town even, without giving either of them a chance to speak.

"What…?" Marcii started, rising to her feet to follow him. But, of course, there was no hope that she would catch him. "Where…?"

Kaylm followed Marcii to the doorway, but Reaper was long gone and there was not a sight nor sound of him to be found.

"Oh Reaper…" Marcii whispered under her breath, sighing, hoping with all her might that he would return.

She breathed deeply and heavily again, feeling the weight of the poor demon's sorrow even in his absence.

"My poor Reaper…I wish you would tell me what's wrong…"

Chapter Thirty-Three

The pair of them paced through the empty streets yet again, side by side, hand in hand, just as any couple should.

Still Reaper had not yet returned. Kaylm did not want to leave until the enormous, protective demon was back with Marcii. He feared for her safety without Reaper to protect her.

They continued to talk as they waited and revelled in having so much time alone together. They had never known such a thing.

Marcii silently suspected that was at least part of the reason for Reaper's seemingly distant nature over the past couple of days.

He was nothing if not caring and respectful. She knew he would have picked up on how she felt about Kaylm, even though she was only just beginning to realise it herself.

Suddenly, out of the corner of her eye, Marcii caught sight of something amidst the grey stone of the buildings.

"What was that?" She asked Kaylm, looking over her shoulder for the movement that had drawn her attention.

"I didn't see anything." Kaylm admitted. "What was it?"

"I don't know…" Marcii breathed, keeping her voice low, though she had no idea really why. "Come on." She urged, striding forwards between the empty buildings. "Let's go see."

Marcii led the way and Kaylm followed, for truly he had not caught a glimpse of anything.

Marcii seemed absolutely convinced that she had however.

She turned and swerved this way and that, looking, searching, but finding no answers.

Then, once again out of the corner of her eye, Marcii caught sight of the same flicker of movement. Her gaze shot over her shoulder and this time swept upwards as it went.

It was barely a second before the movement was gone, but that mere moment was enough.

As Marcii trained her eyes up towards Raven's Keep the figure of a person vanished from sight, disappearing from one of the glassless windows.

"There!" She hissed, pointing up towards the abandoned tower.

"The Keep?" Kaylm questioned, swallowing heavily. "Really?"

"Let's find out." Marcii insisted, dashing from where she stood.

Kaylm didn't need to be asked twice, for his own inquisitions were bubbling. They both surged forward, making directly for the vast tower that stood overlooking the town.

It seemed strange, Marcii thought as they ran, that she hadn't yet been up to the top of the tower.

Raven's Keep was the one place they had both always wanted to come and yet for some reason visiting it had simply not crossed either of their minds.

No matter now though, Marcii thought, as they entered the long, square, stone building at its base. They began ascending the narrow, spiral staircase that wove its way up inside the enormous stone column at the far end of the building.

Marcii's heart raced.

After all these years, the time had finally come. Perhaps it had waited this long for them for a reason.

The pair of them practically burst from the staircase and into the room at the very top of Raven's Keep.

The sight that met them took their breath away.

From the evenly spaced square windows, set every three feet or so in the stone walls, all the way around the huge, circular room, they could see for miles and miles in every direction.

Ravenhead stretched out from the base of the tower in orderly rows of unused houses and mineshafts. The town formed a huge, near perfect circle that seemed to keep close to the tower, afraid to leave.

The town was surrounded on all sides by the greenery of rolling hills and the emptiness of vast plains and the protection of great forests, for as far as the eye could see.

Marcii couldn't believe she was finally here, as she leaned halfway through one of the empty windows and gazed down towards the floor. A hundred and more feet below them the sight was dizzying as she poured her luminous yellow eyes over all that she could see.

Without thinking, for there was simply no need, Kaylm wrapped his arms around Marcii and squeezed her tightly, putting his chin on her shoulder and resting his cheek against hers.

For so long, this was all they had both wanted.

Finally, at long last, they were here.

But, in that wondrous moment, blissfully unaware, they'd both completely forgotten the reason they'd come up here in the first place.

The ghostly figure of a woman with sleek, long, jet black hair, streaked here and there with floods of grey, stood close behind them. She watched the couple curiously with her bright violet eyes, set so deeply into her heavily lined face.

Making not a sound as she moved the woman paced slowed across the wide, circular room and then back again. It was something she had spent many years doing. Her body moved in slow motion without even the tiniest trace of a thought required, for all her attention was set upon Marcii and Kaylm.

The last time she had seen such creatures in her home, her children had been stolen from her.

A strange mixture of emotions swirled inside the ghost of a woman, for she supposed she should really have hated Marcii, but at the same time, she had every reason not to.

It was a bizarre dilemma, to say the least.

Feeling eyes upon her all of a sudden, eyes that had not been there before, only moments ago, Marcii unwound herself nervously from Kaylm's embrace.

He could feel the anxiety in her fingertips and his eyes pooled with worry.

"What is it?" He whispered.

Marcii answered his question only by turning around. She settled her eyes across the other side of the huge room and met Raven's steady gaze with her own.

But still Kaylm did not understand. His eyes swept over to the other side of the perfectly circular stone room and searched the empty abyss laid out before him. After a moment his gaze moved on and glanced all around it again, seeing nothing.

"I don't understand…" He admitted quietly, seeing Marcii's still, focused gaze.

He continued to skim over all that he could see with his own eyes, though clearly he was missing something.

Whether he realised it or not, it didn't matter how hard Kaylm looked, he would not see.

He was just not cut from the same cloth.

The answers they sought would only continue to evade him.

Perhaps that was for the better though.

The answers evaded Marcii too, but they sought at least to give her a mere hint of truth, though without revealing anything significant at all.

"Reaper!" Kaylm suddenly exclaimed, glancing down into the streets below and seeing their enormous demonic friend.

Breaking her concentration for but a mere moment, Marcii stole a glimpse out of the window.

Indeed, it was Reaper. And, strangely, he had a horse.

As he walked the animal trotted contentedly at his side. It had no reigns and he made no attempt to restrain it or stop it from running away. Nevertheless, not once did it part from him, walking close by his thick arm.

Snapping her eyes back across to the other side of the room, to where Raven had just stood, Marcii's stomach sank.

She was gone.

Looking all around, though she knew it would be of no use, Marcii found nothing. She knew that, for now a least, the mysterious ghost of a woman was gone.

Marcii and Kaylm greeted Reaper gladly and he did the same.

"Why have you got a horse?" Marcii asked almost immediately. There was a hint of regret to her voice though, for she thought she could already guess the answer.

Reaper's hands danced his reply.

He told them that the horse was for Kaylm.

"For me?" The young Evans questioned.

Their enormous friend explained that it would get him back to Newmarket faster, and would make his story of having escaped more believable. They had all seen how big he was; surely they would never have believed Kaylm if he'd told them he'd outrun the demon on foot.

"Could the horse outrun you then?" Kaylm asked, though perhaps that wasn't the most pertinent question.

Reaper answered it nonetheless.

With his hands he replied, telling the boy that indeed the horse could not outrun him, but Tyran didn't need to know that. Kaylm nodded his agreement and actually felt a little foolish for asking.

His next question, though it took him another moment or two to pose, was indeed more relevant.

"Why does the horse follow you?" He asked. "Why hasn't it run away?"

But Marcii thought she knew the answer to that query too. Reaper saw her thoughts spark and allowed her to answer for him.

"Reaper has a connection to the world…" Marcii tried to explain. "He feels the ground, and the earth…" She attempted.

Kaylm looked slightly confused, but he listened on, driven, as the best of us are, by curiosity.

"He can feel the world. He can feel nature. It talks to him. It guides him."

Reaper nodded encouragingly.

"And, I suppose, it's not just that…" Marcii continued. "It's more…It's the animals as well…"

Encouragingly, Reaper nodded again and his hands spurred into motion once more.

He congratulated Marcii and confirmed for the both of them that she was right. The horse looked on with half concentrated interest, knowing he had needed to follow Reaper, but knowing not what he was doing with these two humans.

With one of them though, the girl he thought, he could feel a connection similar to that of Reaper's.

From the boy there was nothing.

He was ordinary.

But from her there was definitely something.

The horse wasn't entirely sure what it was, but nonetheless, it was there.

Soon enough, as the day wore inexorably on, Kaylm was well fed and rested. Soon enough he readied himself to depart.

He had yet another long journey ahead of him and he and Marcii both knew that it would be some time before they saw each other again.

If at all.

Marcii's heart grew heavier by the moment and she felt a pit of longing opening up inside of her. The void had always been there, but never quite so infinitely deep.

"Stay safe." She urged of him quietly, her voice barely a whisper as the words quivered off her tongue.

"I will." Kaylm promised, though truth be told he had not the ability to make such statements. "You too."

"I will." Marcii replied. Indeed, her promise, though no more or less sincere than his, carried much more weight behind it, for she had a monstrous demon who would stop at no end to protect her.

Kaylm had nothing of the sort.

Within what felt like only seconds, though truly it was much longer, for she couldn't bear to let him go, Marcii watched as her Kaylm rode off and into the distance.

She tried to stay sturdy, but the sight of him leaving was too much to bear.

Suddenly Marcii faltered and a shaking cry escaped her grasp. Her legs churned beyond her control and carried her forward.

"Kaylm!!" She cried desperately, chasing after him one last time.

He pulled his horse up to stop and turned and jumped down. His feet touched the floor only just in time for Marcii to reach him.

The young Dougherty threw herself at Kaylm and locked her arms tightly around his neck, burying her head into his shoulder.

"Come back to me." She insisted, her voice thick with emotion.

Kaylm nodded but could not speak for he too was laced with love.

Pulling back, but not once releasing the lock of her arms, Marcii gazed into Kaylm's bluey orange eyes for a moment. Her ever glorious yellow gaze held the sight of him, locking onto that image and hoping it would last forever.

She kissed him.

Marcii felt his warm breath inside of her as his lips traced fiercely along hers.

And then, in yet again what felt like a mere moment, Kaylm was gone.

The sight of him disappearing into the distance and off towards the east, fading away between the rolling hills and the trees, made Marcii's heart turn to stone.

He passed between shadows and silhouettes like a ghost, wandering alone through the world without direction, or at least without a hope.

Reaper looked upon the sight with unreadable, jet black eyes, as ever, dark as coal.

As it always had done for those two, absence would forever make their hearts grow fonder.

But this time the odds were stacked heavily against them.

Reaper could quite clearly see the encroaching danger.

As much as they might not want it to, it seemed that now Marcii and Kaylm's long separation would be bridged by much more than merely time.

Chapter Thirty-Four

Malcolm Evans had thought on this for several days now from a hundred different angles, and each time he always eventually came back around to the same conclusion.

His younger brother had defected.

Kaylm was in league with the witch and her demon.

There was no other way about it.

He cursed to himself as he stormed through the narrow, crisscrossing streets of Newmarket, bustling with life and activity as they always were.

He should have known.

The biting air was cold and sharp and stung at his exposed skin.

Where people should have been resting and eating and drinking, making the most of Winter's Dew, they were not.

Instead, as he passed by markets and homes and stalls there came to his ears the ever continuous sound of grindstones and blacksmiths' hammers, forging always new weapons and armour from fresh steel.

Had he an ounce of gentleness in his heart, Kaylm's older brother Malcolm would have seen the wretchedness in all this.

But, sadly, he did not.

And even if he had done, his Lord Tyran would undoubtedly have ripped it from him without a moment's notice, just as the cruel man had done to so many others.

Nonetheless, it was he whom Malcolm was searching for, as he patrolled through the harsh streets.

There were enforcers on every corner. By this point they were an army of huge, unstoppable, armour plated brutes. They all bore the same emblem, somewhere or other, on their brutish weapons and armour. The symbol depicted still the same scene of a person tied to a stake whilst flames licked up all about them.

But the sight of it did not disgust Malcolm.

This was simply what Newmarket had become.

Or, as Lord Tyran constantly assured them all, what Newmarket was made to be.

They could no longer live in fear of monsters hiding in the shadows, attacking and slaughtering innocents in the night.

Malcolm, just the same as everybody else, was only making a stand to protect himself, and his family.

That had included Kaylm, no matter how pathetic he was.

But now, without even any real evidence, Malcolm had decided that Kaylm no longer deserved such protection, and he was about to turn the entirety of Newmarket against him.

In reality though, nothing that had happened in Newmarket of late had been done based on even the tiniest scrap of truth, so this was nothing new.

This was simply the result of Tyran's evil and cruelty seeping out to his underlings, without them even realising it.

Nonetheless, it had worked.

Tyran was in control.

Soon enough Malcolm had found his Lord. As ever, Tyran was surrounded by a host of enforcers, acting more like bodyguards than police.

But Tyran recognised Malcolm as a loyal supporter, for he had never once missed a speech or a hanging or a hunt. Such was Kaylm's older brother's support for his Lord's cause that the dreadful Tyrant even knew him by name.

"Malcolm! My dear boy!" Tyran greeted him from over his enforcers' shoulders. At the dreadful man's mere word, the ominous wall of steel melted from Malcolm's path.

"My Lord." Malcolm greeted Tyran most formally, bowing his head slightly and prostrating himself in every manner short of dropping to his knees and grovelling.

Tyran did not expect that from his subjects.

Not yet anyway.

Such domination was an affliction that Tyran indulged in most willingly and his delusions of grandeur grew with each passing day.

"Enough of the formalities!" Tyran exclaimed, waving his hand as if they mattered not. Of course, he didn't mean what he said, but he wanted to appear at least slightly humble.

Though his body was stout and potbellied, his mind was sharp as a knife and his keen gaze had detected a troubled look in Malcolm's eyes.

The hunt for Marcii and her demon seemed to have dried up.

It was altogether most likely that she was lying face down in a ditch somewhere, having succumbed to the bitter cold weeks ago.

Nonetheless, that was irrelevant, for now Tyran needed something new to satisfy the thirst he had instilled within his lesser people. Simply by the look in Malcolm Evans' eye, he detected that he might have found it.

The disgusting man, cruel though he was, hadn't risen to such realms of wealth and power without having his wits about him, for there is no greater weapon than control of the masses.

"I'm afraid I have troubling news, my Lord." Malcolm stated immediately, his face flickering with grief at what he was having to do.

Tyran's eyes glinted with the promise of bad news, but he did not let it show in his tone, feigning instead deep concern.

"Oh my…" Tyran offered, keeping a straight face, though most insincerely. "What in the world has happened? Come! Sit my boy!"

In an instant, from seemingly nowhere, yet two more enforcers appeared, carrying two chairs between them. The chairs were wooden and handcrafted, each with velvety red cushions sewn onto the seat and up the back.

Though they were in the middle of the market, it mattered not. Tyran simply sat down with Malcolm while his army of enforcers ensured that they were not disturbed.

Curious eyes peered in from this way and that, but the people knew not to get too close, save suffering the heavy blow of a fist or a club to the head.

Tyran's enforcers afforded them almost complete privacy, and of course their own discretion could surely be trusted, for Tyran was lining their pockets endlessly.

"It's my younger brother, Kaylm..." Malcolm confessed. "He never returned from the last hunt..."

"Was he killed?" Tyran asked, narrowing his eyes shrewdly, wondering whether he had misjudged the boy.

But alas, he had not, and Malcolm continued.

"I don't believe so, my Lord." Kaylm's older brother went on. "He hasn't yet returned, but I believe he will..."

"Why do you believe that?" Tyran pressed, cleverly skipping around the real issue of Malcolm's confession, forcing the boy's allegiance to be buried only ever deeper.

"I know him." Malcolm insisted. "He is my brother, after all. And I know he won't want us hunting him."

"And why would we hunt him?" Tyran breathed, unable to help the cruel smile that played across his lips as he spoke, for he could wrap these stupid people up so easily that it was simply too much fun.

"Because he's helping her." Malcolm stated.

"The witch!?" Tyran hissed, faking shock, whilst secretly revelling.

"I'm afraid so…" Malcolm confirmed, nodding solemnly. "He's always been friends with her, no matter how much my parents and I discouraged it…"

"I see…" Tyran noted, nodding his head slowly and seriously, though inwardly he was barely able to contain his excitement. "So…Malcolm…" The cruel Lord continued. "What would you suggest we do?"

He had Malcolm in the palm of his hand.

"Well…I…" Malcolm struggled, searching for the words he thought his Lord wanted to hear. "When he returns, we have to bring him to justice. We can't let him destroy what we fight to protect."

Tyran smiled cruelly.

Malcolm's words sounded as though they had come from his very thoughts.

"I couldn't have said it better myself." Tyran praised the boy. "You are a fine example of a man."

"Thank you, my Lord." Malcolm replied.

"Now…" Tyran pressed. "You have proven to me that you are brave and unfalteringly loyal, Malcolm…"

The young man who was Kaylm's older brother looked up and held his Lord's gaze firmly, knowing that he had condemned Kaylm. But at the same time he was safe from guilt in the knowledge that he had done the right thing.

"Even in the face of your brother's awful defection you have remained on the path of the just and righteous…" He went on.

"Thank you…" Malcolm repeated, though his words faltered somewhat.

Tyran's, however, did not. His voice grew only more grave and more serious.

He made his instruction as plain and as clear as he could possibly manage. He didn't want this idiot misunderstanding his orders.

"When your brother returns, like you said he will…" Malcolm's Lord began slowly, and very purposefully. "I want you to bring him to me. Alive."

Malcolm nodded, but he did not speak.

"Bring him to me." Tyran repeated. "And I promise you his evil ways will not endanger a single soul here. He will be brought to justice."

"Yes my Lord." Malcolm confirmed, fully understanding his task, knowing that it was for the good of the people.

He could not allow the evil witch Marcii to claim any more innocent lives, no matter if that meant dealing with his brother in order to do so.

"Good." Tyran breathed. "Very good. Now, in the meantime…"

His words pressed on menacingly, driving, and his eyes glinted dreadfully.

"Prepare for war…"

All those who heard Tyran's orders, as far as he was aware, were enforcers.

They belonged to him.

He had nothing to worry about.

But what he did not know, for there was absolutely no way he could have done, was that a certain little girl, posing as a poor, homeless, helpless orphan, overlooked by all, was listening to his every word. With twigs strewn through her light brown hair that fell down haphazardly to cover her tawny eyes, Vixen stood in the background, hidden amidst the shadows.

She listened to Tyran's orders with grim determination.

Marcii was about to lose everything.

The girl who looked to be a young orphan set immediately into motion.

Vixen could not warn Kaylm; that was not possible.

But she could warn Marcii, and warn her she would.

Without such grace, Marcii, Kaylm, and indeed Reaper too, would surely all suffer the same fate.

Though Kaylm might have been returning with the hope of misdirecting any future hunts, little did he know how drastically different his own family's agenda was, and that his efforts would be all but futile.

It was down to Vixen to intervene.

But then, that was nothing new, for that was her entire purpose in life.

Besides, just as she wasn't what she appeared to be, the task that lay now once again at her feet wasn't all that great of a burden.

It was not with her that the heaviest weight lay.

No.

Truly, that lay with the young Marcii Dougherty.

Chapter Thirty-Five

There was an entire network of tunnels that ran endlessly beneath the abandoned streets of Ravenhead, crisscrossing at a hundred and more intersections in the darkness.

Rails that used to ferry innumerable carts ran through the thick dirt, buried beneath many years of sediment and decay. But then as the rails descended deeper into the tunnels, pervading the mines as they went, the dirt turned swiftly to cold, hard rock.

Odd, abandoned carts decorated the tracks here and there randomly, unused for so many years.

They had been so heavily relied upon that the metal rails had been pinned into the very stone with thick, foot long bolts, and remained there even still, unchanged after all this time.

It was nearly pitch black as Marcii navigated her way slowly through the never ending tunnels, only able to do so because by now her eyes were so well adjusted to the veil of darkness. Nonetheless, Reaper still walked with her. The tunnels were so enormous and so ingrained that for the most part he barely even needed to duck.

There were one to two points however, as they passed through the limitless blackness, where even Marcii was forced to stoop, and Reaper had to drop to his hands and knees and crawl.

It was the first time Marcii had been down in the tunnels since coming to Ravenhead. Her breath steamed out in front of her in the cold of the shafts in steady, nervous billows.

Marcii placed her feet in her soft leather shoes as deftly as she could manage either side of the thick, metal rails, and occasionally found herself walking along them, her arms outstretched as if she were walking a tightrope.

They had found a whole new world down there. It was a place where the air was perpetually cold. Where sound echoed round in circles forever, unable to escape. Where you could flee from the horrors of the world above and quite easily never again be found.

But, hard as she tried, and deep as she and Reaper ventured, Marcii could not escape.

All the while her mind swam with thoughts of Kaylm.

No matter what she did, or how fast she moved, or how deep she went, she was ceaselessly distracted.

It had been not even three days since Kaylm had left Ravenhead.

Marcii imagined that, although he would have had to make his way around the canyon, because Kaylm was on horseback, he would more than likely arrive back at Newmarket that very day.

She hoped with all her might that he would be well received.

Undoubtedly his family would have something to say about his disappearance.

Little did she know of the harsh reality Kaylm was yet to face.

They continued through the pitch black of the mining tunnels and eventually Reaper began to lead her back towards the surface.

Without Reaper's perfect eyesight, or his unique connection with the earth that allowed him such flawless navigation, Marcii would surely have been lost forever down there.

After what felt like a lifetime they emerged back into the cold, bright day. Though the sky was clear and perfect blue, it was much colder out here than it had been down in the mines.

Regardless of the weather outside however, the temperature in the tunnels was forever constant.

Nonetheless, Marcii couldn't imagine the thought of living down there for the rest of her life. On the contrary, Reaper had taken quite a liking to them, whilst the young Dougherty had begun restoring one of the homes that still had a standing roof.

To say restoring was perhaps generous.

She'd spent some time clearing rubble from the floor, making it more comfortable to sleep on. She'd also emptied the fire pit in the centre of the room to make space for it to be used properly.

If Reaper was to sleep in the mines and she was to sleep here, she would most certainly need a fire.

Much was changing it seemed.

The only thing that remained constant were Marcii's endless thoughts of Kaylm and how she missed him so.

But then, all of a sudden, as Marcii scooped another pile of rubble from the floor to clear the doorway, her head spun unexpectedly and her vision went blurred and hazy.

She knew at once what was happening and she cried out to try to warn Reaper as she fell forward.

It mattered not though, for it was already too late.

Marcii's body fell from her grasp as her mind was whisked off elsewhere.

Rubble scattered all over the floor as she fell, but Marcii did not see it.

At first, just as before, the world went black.

Then, when her head finally stopped spinning, she felt herself lying flat on the ground.

Once again Marcii could not see or hear a thing. Eventually the oppressive haze in her mind cleared and the young Dougherty found herself staring up at the bright, sunny blue sky, with the sound of chatter and footsteps all around her.

The ground was hard but oddly warm in the heat of the afternoon sun. Marcii's head rested on rough cobblestones and throbbed heavily from where she'd fallen.

Just inches from her head, every few seconds, heavy footsteps barely missed her face.

It was only a matter of time before a weighty boot came down directly upon her.

Marcii was still too dizzy to move out of the way, even instinctively. She flinched the first time, but when the person's shoe and foot passed straight through her again, she relaxed slightly, knowing nobody knew she was there.

Nonetheless, as she sat slowly up, nerves flooded through the young Dougherty's veins, afraid of what she might find.

The streets teemed with bustling life as people hurried to and fro merrily, laughing and joking and smiling as they went. Marcii frowned for a moment, wondering what was going on.

Had something changed?

She saw no enforcers.

There were no market stalls.

No hint of tyranny.

But then, as she glanced up towards the blinding blue ocean of sky above, she realised all of a sudden why.

This was not Newmarket.

This was Ravenhead.

Chapter Thirty-Six

Wandering through the streets, passing perfectly through strangers as she went, Marcii marvelled at the busy sights all around her.

Though it was exactly the same town, for the buildings and streets were all unchanged and identical, save being in better condition, Marcii barely recognised the place. She had only ever known it to be abandoned and to see it now teeming with life was most bizarre.

There were not the shouts of commerce echoing about that she had grown up with though. All the stores here seemed to be inside buildings with doors and windows, filled with glass that had black, perfectly spaced writing printed across them.

Marcii sensed an air of sophistication that she also wasn't accustomed to, though not to the point of being pompous. People passed by in every direction talking in deep conversation about all manner of things, but were not rude to their fellow townsfolk and often smiled or waved at each other.

One name seemed to crop up more than most, Marcii noticed, as she passed through the streets and people like a ghost, and that name was Raven.

Almost instinctively, stopping and turning quite purposefully, Marcii looked up to Raven's Keep. She caught her breath as her eyes fell upwards, for the tower too was filled with life.

Sweeping through the hectic streets with new purpose Marcii strode straight through solid stone and wood, heading directly for the vast column that jutted up into the warm skies.

She caught glimpses every now and then of a figure passing by the windows in the tower, and though they were mere glances, Marcii knew exactly who it was.

It was the same woman she had seen in the tower, only a few days previous, before Kaylm had left.

Raven.

For some reason Kaylm had not been able to see her, but Marcii had.

She'd vanished before Marcii had been given chance to get any answers. But here she was again in her vision and the young Dougherty was determined to find her.

Marcii raced up the twisting spiral staircase, not the first time, charging straight through all who stood in her path.

She felt her heart racing, beating faster and faster by the second. For some reason she was afraid and excited all at once.

She knew who she would find when she reached the top, so close now.

But for some reason, though she couldn't quite understand why, Marcii felt as if there was much more to come.

After barely a few more seconds she burst into the perfectly circular room atop the tower.

Sure as the day is long, there she was.

The mysterious woman Raven paced the huge room back and forth, her hands clasped gently behind her back as she strode, slowly and wistfully.

Raven was indeed, just as the folktales had always ensured Marcii, and just as she had seen a few days before, stunning.

She was aged, clearly, for her face was deeply lined.

It was much easier for Marcii to see now that she wasn't merely a ghost.

The woman's bright, violet eyes were youthful, though her years showed heavily upon the rest of her. Her straight, jet black hair was streaked even still with varying shades of grey, though not so greatly as Marcii remembered from the other day.

Suddenly, as Raven turned and the light streaming in from the windows caught her aged face in a particular way, Marcii's breath caught in her chest.

She was the spitting image of Malorie.

Her eyes. Her hair. Her face. Even the way she moved.

It was too similar for Marcii to ignore. A lump lodged in her throat as she tried to speak.

But then, as if to answer her very question, the next person to appear behind her, having ascended the spiral stairs all but silently, was Malorie herself.

The strange, beautiful woman whom Marcii had known almost her entire life, though in reality now dead, looked youthful and free from the heavy weight of burden. Her eyes were an identical, luminous violet to Raven's, though her own jet black hair showed no streaks of any other colour.

Neither of them spoke and they didn't look at Marcii, for of course they had no idea she was there.

Well, as far as Marcii knew at least, she wasn't there.

But she couldn't really have said that for sure.

She still didn't know exactly what was happening, or what her strange visions meant.

Nonetheless, they were growing clearer, firmer, if those were the best words to use.

She couldn't think of any other way to describe them.

They just felt more real.

All of a sudden, realising she'd been lost in thought, Marcii snapped back to reality, or not, as the case might have been, and set her eyes upon Raven again.

But now the sound of joy and laughter was gone. As Marcii peered out curiously upon the streets below, frowning, she saw they were desolate once again.

Glancing around, confused, Malorie was gone. She was alone with Raven.

Or perhaps with the memory of Raven.

The young Dougherty couldn't fathom it.

It all seemed so real that surely it had to be the truth.

But it didn't make any sense.

Raven turned again, pacing now even more slowly than she had been before. Though of course Marcii didn't catch her eye, she could see that the beautiful, aged woman's face was stricken beyond belief.

Endless sorrow poured down her heavily lined cheeks and filled the deep creases in her face with laden sadness.

Marcii took a breath to speak, hoping desperately to somehow rouse Raven's attention, but she was too late.

Suddenly her vision was interrupted by another scene altogether. It was something infinitely more overwhelming, though equally as powerful, just in a different way.

In the space of a fleeting heartbeat Marcii was no longer in the tower, silent and undisturbed and surrounded by emptiness.

Instead she found herself amidst a roaring, surging, screaming crowd. The sound shocked and deafened her and barraged her thoughts uncaringly.

She recognised the sound and indeed too the place.

She was back in Newmarket.

But that wasn't what drew the young Dougherty's attention, for there was something else that struck at her heart more than all else.

Not just something else, but indeed someone else.

Someone too that she recognised.

Someone that she loved, and he was in grave danger.

Kaylm.

Chapter Thirty-Seven

Marcii could only stand by a watch helplessly. To see Kaylm suffer left a pit of emptiness in her stomach that the young Dougherty simply could not fill.

Abandoned and apprehended all at once, Kaylm was down on his knees in the centre of the square.

Tyran presided over the dreadful sight, but it was Kaylm's own family who stood watchfully over him, ensuring he could not escape.

His parents, Victoria and Stephen Evans, wore expressions of disappointment and grave regret. Not only had their son betrayed them, and indeed the rest of Newmarket too, but he had likely been helping the witches all along. He might not even have realised it at the time, but Kaylm had been at least partly responsible for the deaths of all those murdered by the demon Reaper.

They were so ashamed.

Malcolm stood off a way, Marcii saw, and the look upon his face was different to that of his parents'.

Whilst he looked disappointed, just as they did, Malcolm's expression was tinged also with something else: something that resembled a very sombre picture of pride and duty.

It looked much less like pride to Marcii though, and a lot more like betrayal, as is sadly all too common amongst families.

In an instant, before anything else even need happen, Marcii knew without a shadow of a doubt that Malcolm was the one responsible for this.

She screamed and bellowed and roared in anger, charging forwards, filled to bursting with endless, love driven fury. But it didn't matter how loudly Marcii shrieked, nor how far her wild cries carried, Malcolm didn't hear her.

Neither did Kaylm.

His head drooped further and further as his energy and his will and even his very life drained slowly away, melting down through the cold stone below him.

His face was black and blue once again. Blood trickled from his chin and stained his clothes and the ground beneath him.

Finally quieting her shrieks, for they were futile, Marcii gathered both her breath and her wits and paced over to Kaylm.

She knelt down to look him in the eye with her brimming gaze.

He couldn't see her of course, but Marcii could see him.

The sight tore at the strings of her heart.

Kaylm murmured and tried to look up.

Marcii's heart leapt for a moment, but it was soon knocked back down. As Kaylm looked up, his gaze blurred and dizzied, Malcolm swept in like a vulture. He was bigger and broader and stronger than Kaylm, as he always had been.

He lifted his hand almost casually to strike his younger brother back down.

Blood sprayed in every direction, spattering the cobblestones and the front rows of the crowd.

Marcii screamed again. Again though, her cries went all but unheard throughout Newmarket, as the crowds roared and cheered with excitement.

Back in Ravenhead however, where her body still resided, there was one who heard Marcii's cries. Her writhing body was strewn across the rubble lined floor and she was bleeding from a cut across her forehead.

Reaper sensed Marcii's distress, seeing quite clearly that something was wrong.

Clouds swarmed above the abandoned town and swirled in unnatural patterns, centring directly above where Marcii lay. The winds picked up harshly and cut through Reaper's enormous body most unusually like a knife.

He didn't feel the shrill cold, not even a little bit. But he knew that regardless of whatever might be happening to Marcii, whether she was conscious or not, it would strike ice into her very veins.

The elements stirred furiously, but then so did Marcii, and Mother Nature responded in kind.

Flashes of lighting tore through the swarming black sea above and a symphony of thunder rang across the skies for miles in every direction.

Just as the weather in Ravenhead turned and writhed, the skies above Newmarket charred angrily above Kaylm's head, mirroring the image cast so many miles away. The young Evans glanced upwards briefly, seeing the clouds thrash and churn, not knowing that Marcii was by his side even still.

Malcolm struck his younger brother across the face once more and the crowds cheered again, even more fiercely than before. Kaylm's head dropped back down and he squeezed his eyes tightly shut against the pain, though he made not a peep of a sound.

Lightning cracked furiously and lighted the anger flashing in Marcii's eyes.

She didn't even notice the weather flickering and teetering on her every whim, changing in lieu with her rushing emotions. By that point she'd become so used to it that she barely noticed the black, swelling ocean above her rise and screech and roar so dreadfully.

Hail suddenly ripped from the thick clouds and cascaded down like enormous lumps of alien rock, pelting the ground and everybody mortal residing upon it.

Newmarket squirmed beneath the barrage and everyone scurried off in all directions to find shelter from the onslaught.

All but Kaylm rushed to find protection, for he was still bound down upon his knees. There was nothing he could do as the hail bombarded him relentlessly, striking his already battered body.

Only Marcii stayed with him, though of course the hailstones passed straight through her and shattered against the cobblestoned ground directly beneath her.

Tears coursed helplessly down her face.

She could only look on at her Kaylm as the stones struck him relentlessly. Ironically, and indeed rather tragically, it was by her own hand that now he suffered from the harsh elements, whether she realised it or not.

Regardless, what he was now enduring undoubtedly had saved him from a much worse fortune.

That strange twist of fate had perhaps even saved his life.

For a few more moments Marcii looked on, quivering terribly.

But then another emotion struck her, quite literally, as searing pain coursed through her face.

A hailstone hit Marcii's forehead, right above her eye.

She was instantly blinded and she recoiled back from it, crying out with pain.

The young Dougherty didn't even have chance to consider how that was possible, as more hailstones crashed into her, striking her fragile body all over.

All of a sudden she felt the cold, hard ground beneath her as she lay on her back. She could only presume that she'd fallen beneath the heavy barrage raining down upon her.

Then a huge, impending silhouette loomed over her, blocking out the light, but at the same time shielding her from the vicious onslaught of hard ice.

Raising her weary hands to protect her face Marcii cracked her eyes open cautiously, fearful of what she might find. The enormous black shadow was blurred at first and she could only make out its outline, standing over her, shielding her from her own creation.

Her entire body pounded with searing pain.

Eventually her eyes began to focus and the details of the demon's immense body came to sight.

"Reaper…?" The young Dougherty breathed, barely able to talk. Her voice croaked and groaned as the sound left her, as if it would never come back.

As if something was lost forever.

The enormous demon's hands flickered above Marcii's face, dancing at a rate that seemed impossible to follow, let alone understand.

But, naturally, even in her dazed state, only just coming around from whatever it was that had once again engulfed her, Marcii fully understood Reaper's words.

Of course, as he always would, he asked her if she was okay.

Marcii looked around for a moment, stunned by everything that was happening.

Eventually she nodded, frantically and erratically, though she wasn't even really sure herself.

Reaper helped her slowly to her feet, sheltering her all the while as hailstones smashed into the ground all around them and shattered into millions of pieces.

The heavy shards of ice hammered into Reaper's vast shoulders and back, glancing off in every direction as they did so.

But they did not harm him.

He quickly half led and half carried Marcii into the tunnels for shelter.

The sound of the storm followed them inescapably inside. It reverberated all around as if the hailstones were yet even still falling about them.

Marcii's face was red and it took her a minute or two to come to her wits. But when she finally did, breathing deeply, she looked at Reaper with deep, pooling eyes that swam in unimaginable worry.

"Reaper…" She eventually breathed, though this time her voice did not shake and quiver quite so badly.

The enormous demon's hands spun into motion, asking her what she'd seen. Asking her what had happened. Asking her if she was okay.

Just by the look in Marcii's eyes however, for they were beyond haunted, Reaper had no real need for his questions.

Though her quivering voice might have recovered, that troubled gaze of hers was filled with all sorts of rushing emotions.

"Kaylm…" She breathed. "They've got Kaylm…I have to go back to Newmarket…" Her whispered words were thick with emotion. "They're going to kill him…"

Chapter Thirty-Eight

Reaper saw much more than Marcii did.

But only for now, he thought sombrely.

It wasn't a matter of whether or not Marcii's power would grow now, it was simply a matter of time.

She was already doing more than she could possibly even imagine.

The enormous demon could see all of this quite clearly by now: much more than the young Dougherty could. He knew there was little he could do other than wait. He still knew that he wouldn't be the one to reveal such things to her, for it was not his place.

All would be revealed soon enough.

It had to be, he considered silently, as his enormous legs carried him at terrifying speeds across the great plains and through the forests. He bounded further and further with every step and the wind ripped around him as he went.

They were heading straight into the lion's den. It would take much more than simple chance if they were going to come out alive.

But, undoubtedly, Reaper had already seen much more than chance at work over the past months.

Though she might not have known it yet, Marcii was in the safest hands possible.

He just hoped that would be enough.

He had seen it be plenty before now.

But then, equally, he had seen it go disastrously wrong too.

Attempting to keep his racing thoughts in check, for they had run away with him more than a few times of late, the monstrous demon focused on the task at hand.

The crystal clear, perfect blue sky was only just beginning to darken in the late afternoon as Reaper crossed the land at an unreal pace. When they'd left, wasting not a single moment, Marcii was certain that Reaper wouldn't be able to maintain his ridiculous stride. But indeed he had, and he seemed not in the least bit fatigued.

Within what felt like only hours they were far away from Ravenhead once more, tearing through trees and around vast lakes and plains as Reaper ran only ever faster.

The weather flickered and changed even still as Marcii's thoughts raced too, and as her emotions swarmed inside of her.

Because of the biting cold the huge hailstones that had fallen earlier still kicked up about Reaper's feet in flurrying blizzards.

Despite his size his huge strides made almost no sound as the enormous demon crisscrossed the landscape, heading always perfectly east, straight for Newmarket.

More and more hours passed and Marcii was grateful for Reaper's warmth as he held her, for though she could feel the icy chill of the wind as he ran, it did not touch her.

Eventually, after what felt like a very long night, Reaper finally slowed. He didn't stop though and continued on at a brisk walk, shifting Marcii's weight onto one arm as he did so.

His free hand came up to the young Dougherty's eye line and flickered into motion, asking her first and foremost if she was okay.

Marcii nodded and Reaper continued.

She quickly realised that he'd slowed to warn her.

They were approaching the canyon.

He assured her there was nothing to fear, and not to panic.

"What do you mean?" Marcii asked, her voice cutting through the cold night like a knife.

Her enormous demon explained that he would not slow down, but that she would be perfectly safe.

Marcii's stomach turned and knotted slightly and she only managed a nod in reply.

Reaper knew that the longer he left it now the more apprehensive she would become. And so, taking off immediately at another dead run, he moved somehow even faster than before.

All too soon the canyon reared up before them with frightening speed and certainty.

Without even breaking his stride Reaper raced for the edge. At first it didn't seem to Marcii like he was even going to jump.

Her stomach balled into a tight fist.

He hadn't bothered to aim for a narrower section of the canyon, for he knew it would not matter.

At the very last moment, pushing off from one foot as he ran, placing his last step unnervingly close to the edge, all of a sudden they were airborne.

The ground disappeared.

The world seemed suddenly to be infinitely bigger than ever before and a vast pit of blackness stretched out endlessly beneath them.

Marcii held her breath, though for some reason she couldn't bring herself to close her eyes, as she gazed out at the world seemingly so far below.

Compared to last time Reaper had done this, though her apprehension had been similar, now the fear didn't grip her so.

She felt as if they sailed a giant arc through the air in glorious slow motion.

Life seemed to pass by below her in the never ending darkness, in that spectacular moment, as if it were without time. Endless generations stretched out before her, secluded in pitch blackness.

Simply existing, but certainly not living.

All too soon Reaper's feet touched the ground again, but instead of crashing down onto two feet, his momentum was such that he landed without breaking his pace. Setting one foot down in front of his enormous body, his legs churned immediately and they were back off running again.

Marcii marvelled at the magnificent creature, going to such lengths for her, when he needn't have done any of the things he had for her over the past months.

Truth be told, whilst Reaper had not wanted to go back to Ravenhead, now that he had done, it had struck him agonisingly to leave again.

Through young Marcii's heart and chest her emotions stirred and flurried endlessly. Forevermore though they would also wreak havoc through

Reaper's enormous body, ripping him to shreds from the inside out.

During that night, as Ravenhead fell further and further away into the distance, and as Newmarket grew ever closer and closer, the monstrous demon was perhaps more human than most, and he felt it all too keenly in the endless darkness.

Chapter Thirty-Nine

Lights appeared in the distance, flickering and uncertain in the night.

They seemed to dance and move in Marcii's vision as they drew nearer, but that was due more to the bobbing motion of Reaper's enormous strides, than that they were indeed jumping between windows.

As they crested yet another rolling hill beneath the vast ocean of worlds floating above them, Marcii sighed pensively.

It was early morning and they had made exquisite time thanks to Reaper's relentless pace. He didn't seem even in the least bit fatigued.

Marcii doubted she would ever see him so.

But then, nothing is impossible, she thought.

As a matter of fact, the young Dougherty had pondered on quite a number of things throughout the duration of their hasty journey. Most of all, as ever, she thought of Kaylm, hoping desperately that they weren't too late.

She hadn't had any more visions, so she knew no more than she had done the previous afternoon.

Suddenly, interrupting her swirling notions, Reaper stopped dead, unmoving for a moment.

He crouched low, bending down slowly, surveying the blackness laid out before and all around them with piercing coal eyes.

Marcii held her breath.

Her eyes were adjusted to the night, as they often were these days, but she knew in comparison to Reaper she could likely still see very little.

In fact, she had no idea what he was looking at.

All she could do was wait.

Without warning Reaper raced immediately into motion again, sweeping Marcii along with him.

His enormous strides carried them silently down the front side of the hill they had just crested. They fell within seconds into the deep shadow of the landscape, away from the exposing skyline, and into a dense copse situated below.

"Reaper!" Marcii hissed through clenched, fearful teeth. "What is it?"

But the enormous demon just set her quietly down at the base of a massive tree and brought one enormous finger up to his lips. His hands wove a quick message, warning her that they were not alone.

Marcii opened her mouth to ask if it was Tyran's men, but caught her tongue just in time, heeding her friend's warning to remain quieted.

Straining her eyes through the darkness, scanning as best she could between the trees for the shapes of men and the flicker of torches amidst the night, it took Marcii some time to realise that she was looking for something that wasn't there.

She glanced up at Reaper to find that his expression was steely and grim: more so than she had ever seen it.

Without any idea what he could see that she couldn't, Marcii continued to survey the hills and the fields and the forests, unsure exactly what she should be searching for.

Suddenly, between the shadows and the moonshine that cast down here and there, she saw a figure loping slowly across the land, keeping low to the ground.

Then another.

And another.

Each one followed the last in a slow, steady procession, fanning out across the fields and between the thick trees in set, organised patterns.

They moved on four legs and looked perfectly at home in the wilderness.

Whatever they were, they were not of Newmarket, and most certainly did not belong upon its streets.

But, nonetheless, that's where they seemed to be heading, making a beeline straight for the town through the heavy night.

"What are they?" Marcii whispered under her breath, her voice barely even breaking the silence for it was so quiet.

Reaper's panicked hand shot out immediately to cover the sound and he pushed her down low to the ground. He practically threw himself flat to the floor too and Marcii daren't even breathe, terrified.

Her heart leapt and skipped several beats as fear coursed through her.

She had never seen Reaper act so.

She bit her tongue harshly, knowing by his flurried actions that she had severely endangered them both by disobeying him.

Remaining silent with her head pressed down low to the ground, Marcii could do nothing but wait, hoping desperately that her actions would not have dire repercussions.

Eventually, though Marcii had no idea how much time had passed, Reaper at last rose from the floor to crouch. He helped Marcii to her feet and immediately his hands wove an apology for throwing her down.

Marcii nodded to say that she understood and to apologise, but she daren't speak again: not until she knew it was safe to do so.

After what felt like another lifetime Reaper finally smiled and nodded encouragingly, ensuring her that it was safe.

"What was it?" The young Dougherty asked, her voice still hushed and shaky.

Reaper knelt on one knee and wove words with his hands in the night.

His soundless explanation told Marcii that it was something he'd hoped they would not have to face and even in his fingers alone Marcii could see the great demon's fear.

Marcii opened her mouth to ask another question, for still she didn't know what she'd seen, but she could tell by Reaper's rushed motions that they had very little time.

The concern that scurried through his enormous body was all too obvious.

"Let's go." Marcii suggested quickly, hoping that the sooner they rescued Kaylm, the sooner they could return to the safety of Ravenhead.

Reaper saw the logic in Marcii's eyes and heard it in her words.

He smiled as warmly and as convincingly as he could manage.

Unfortunately, as much as he may have been trying to comfort Marcii, he could not escape the truth that resided in his own mind.

The enormous, dreadful demon knew that now, no matter what happened, there was no escaping what lay immediately in their path.

If they continued into Newmarket to try to save Kaylm, if he was even still alive, they would be putting themselves in grave danger.

If things were as bad as he feared, it was altogether possible that they might not return.

And then, even if they did, despite all the odds that were stacked so heavily against them, they may very well find that they did not return alone.

Chapter Forty

Marcii crept slowly from shadow to shadow, keeping low and out of sight as much as she could manage.

She was alone, for Reaper had not come with her.

He had instructed her to hide, and quite firmly so. His words had not danced around the point. He had warned her that what they were doing was very dangerous and that, if she were to be faced by anyone, or anything, she was not to confront them.

He would be watching and listening intently.

Without him, clearly, she would be able to find Kaylm more quickly. She knew these streets; he did not. And besides, she would be able to move more quickly and more safely without a great, hulking demon trailing behind her.

She was to get Kaylm and get out.

Those were her instructions.

Nonetheless, Marcii was unable to shake the concern so evident in Reaper's words from her mind, even as she slunk through the familiar, narrow streets.

It was strange to be back.

The rotting stench of the cat carcasses finally seemed to have faded. She hoped for pity's sake they had at long last been removed.

Here and there hailstones were still cast about the floor. Most of them had been kicked to the sides of the streets and alleys to clear pathways for carts, but a few still skittered away from Marcii's feet as she stole through the darkness.

There were very few people that Marcii saw, though when she did it was always too close a call for comfort.

Marcii felt decidedly vulnerable, for she was all too aware that this was not a vision, and indeed that she would most certainly be seen if she was not careful. She stole through the night like a ghost, as many people often seem to.

For the most part those she saw were enforcers. The young Dougherty held her breath every time she hid, slinking as far back into the shadows as she could possibly manage, feeling a fresh, familiar fear filling her chest.

Fortunately, such close encounters were few and far between. She swept on silent feet through the ruined town and towards the square. She was heading, naturally, into Newmarket's very heart, for she needed to find the worst her old home had to offer, as undoubtedly that was where Kaylm would be.

Or so she hoped at least.

Shudders ran up and down her spine, interlocked with shivers that laced her very bones. The weather was bitterly cold, but Marcii wasn't sure whether she was feeling it so because the air had turned even harsher, or simply because she was without Reaper's encompassing warmth.

She felt decidedly lost without the enormous demon at her side and frequently glanced behind her to glimpse his face, only to find that he was not there.

Sighing, the young Dougherty pressed on, forcing her stiff, freezing body to keep moving, searching all the while for her Kaylm.

The square drew nearer and the fearful wind grew harsher, lashing at Marcii with icy fingers. She pulled the sheepskin pelt that she still wore more tightly around her neck and shoulders, fighting to keep the chill at bay.

A sudden sound drew Marcii's attention and she instinctively shrunk back into the depths of the shadows in the nearest alleyway.

Someone was approaching.

As far as she could tell there were three sets of footsteps, perhaps four.

Holding her breath again, afraid to make even the slightest sound, she curled up into a ball in the coldest, darkest, dankest corner that she had found all night and waited for them to pass.

Their silhouettes flitted in and out of her sight in barely the space of a single heartbeat, and aside from their light, clanking footsteps striking the uneven cobblestones, they made not a sound in the frightful night.

Once they had passed and the sound of their footsteps faded off into the night Marcii detached herself from the shadows in which she had concealed herself.

She didn't notice the single, lonesome figure that loomed up behind her as she did so.

All but unaware, the young Dougherty peered out into the now empty street once again, checking to see if her path was clear.

Unmoving, the silhouette stood close behind watched her closely, making not a sound.

After a few moments, ready to set off again, Marcii prepared to dart out into the street and cross to the shadowy alleys on the other side.

Suddenly though, just as her legs coiled into springs, a voice like thunder sounded and cut through the silence like death.

Marcii's heart and legs both faltered and her stomach caved in at the sound, for she'd had no idea there was somebody behind her. She felt as though she'd been punched in the gut by fear itself as the voice struck her.

"Don't." Was all it said.

Without even the breath to scream in shock, for her chest felt as if her lungs had collapsed, Marcii half crumpled and half turned, raising her hands instinctively to protect herself.

Her eyes flashed in the darkness and immediately met the gaze that had been observing her.

Recognition followed her shock and Marcii stammered to speak.

"Hush." The young orphan's voice breathed then, rushing to Marcii's side and cupping her tiny, child sized hand over her mouth.

"Vixen!?" Marcii hissed, shaking off the girl's hand, though the rest of her words failed her at first, for her heart still skittered to a frantic, terrified rhythm.

"Hush." Vixen urged again, but Marcii was not listening.

"Vixen!" She repeated, though more harshly this time. "What the…!?"

But she was not allowed to finish.

Vixen's hand clamped over Marcii's mouth more firmly: far too firmly for a mere child.

"Shut up!" The young orphan instructed, cracking her words like a whip. Reluctantly, Marcii obeyed, somehow unable to shake the girl off.

They glared at each other for a moment, but Marcii daren't utter another sound. After a few seconds, allowing a moment for the air to settle, it was the young orphan girl who spoke again.

"You're in terrible danger." Vixen warned. "You have to come with me."

"No!" Marcii suddenly burst out. "I'm not going anywhere with you! Not until you tell me what the hell is going on!"

Vixen just looked at Marcii as if her ranting was entirely irrelevant. But Marcii continued nonetheless.

"Why do you keep showing up!?" The young Dougherty demanded. "How do you know I'm in danger!? How do you always know where I am!? How do you know any of this!?"

"Marcii…" Vixen attempted, but she wasn't listening.

"No!" Marcii demanded again, this time refusing to back down. "I want to know!"

All of a sudden, completely out of the blue, Vixen did something Marcii certainly hadn't been expecting.

In a single, swift, unseen movement, unconcealed and yet barely visible all at once, she drew her hand quickly up and slapped Marcii sharply across the face. Combined with the icy cold air and the chill wind, the slap stung harshly, stealing Marcii's breath from her.

"Shut up." Vixen breathed again, this time more fiercely, though her voice was much lower and much quieter. "There isn't time for this now. If you go out there, you will die."

Vixen glanced out into the desolate street as she spoke and chills crawled menacingly up Marcii's back, clawing hungrily at her spine.

"But…" Marcii began, thrown from her furious demands without success.

Vixen simply wouldn't have it.

"Enough!" The young orphan snapped, flitting her gaze once again between her Dougherty and the empty street beyond the alley. She stormed past Marcii and forced open a locked door, ramming it heavily with her shoulder so that the lock burst inwards.

Marcii couldn't believe what she was seeing.

"Vixen…?" She started, but the young orphan still wasn't listening.

"Get inside!" She ordered. "If you ever want to see Kaylm again, get inside!"

Struck by the finality in Vixen's tone, sending fear fleeting through her veins, Marcii complied and scurried inside behind the tiny orphan.

Vixen closed the door immediately and forced a wooden chair beneath the handle, ensuring it would stay shut.

"What's going on?" Marcii asked again, but again Vixen silenced her.

"Quiet!" The little girl hissed, pushing Marcii down by her shoulders and out of sight of the window that overlooked the empty street outside through dirty glass.

Marcii had no idea what was going on, but Vixen was terrifying her.

She did as she was instructed, making not a sound.

For a moment nothing happened, but Vixen still did not move. The young girl kept them both crouched low, perfectly still, below the line of the filthy window.

Suddenly a silhouette appeared in the street outside, moving slowly on all fours, keeping low to the ground. The massive shadowy figure loped deliberately past the grimy glass, filling it with blackness for a moment, blocking out all of the light.

Marcii was filled immediately with dread, horrified by what she saw.

She didn't know what it was.

But she daren't speak until the beast had passed.

The shadow eventually loped out of view, vanishing from sight of the window and disappearing down the street without a sound.

"Follow me." Vixen finally breathed, standing up again, signalling that, at least for now, the danger had passed.

"What was that?" Marcii whispered, afraid to even do that.

"They're wolves." Vixen answered, not even looking back as she slunk through the house, passing in and out of the tiny kitchen without a sound.

Marcii struggled to believe that.

Though it wasn't quite the size of Reaper, the gigantic figure had looked more like a bear than a wolf.

But before Marcii could say another word, as a plague of terrified notions ran flurrying through her mind, the sound of distant howls echoed through the dark of the night.

They were a dreadful, chilling sound that resonated around Newmarket like cries of war.

Even Vixen's face dropped at the noise and Marcii could see the same dread fill the young orphan like a deathly poison.

"We have to go." Vixen breathed. "Now."

"Is it safe?" Marcii asked, her voice quaking, though for some reason she trusted Vixen's judgement completely.

Unfortunately, whilst that might have been true, Vixen was nothing if not honest.

"No." The young orphan admitted. "Not in the slightest. But if we don't go now, Kaylm will die."

Chapter Forty-One

Clear in the blackness of the night, Marcii's face turned a ghostly shade of white.

"We have to go." Vixen breathed, wrenching the front door to the house they'd broken into open without a sound. "Now."

Without giving Marcii chance to respond Vixen took off at a dead run from the doorway, leaving the door wide open behind her.

Fear surged through her veins as the young Dougherty lurched after the young, orphaned girl, chasing her for not the first time through Newmarket and yet still unable to catch her.

Suddenly Marcii's ears were filled with the sounds of screams and fierce barking. The sounds reverberated all around in the night and created a symphony of suffering for all to hear.

Vixen tore down the streets and alleyways without even pausing to think and Marcii trailed after her, trying desperately to keep up.

She was moving inhumanly fast, seeming to know where both man and beast were going to be even before they did. With her strange, impossible knowledge, Vixen managed to lead Marcii through the very heart of the carnage.

Enormous wolves tore at the skin and bone of Newmarket's people, ripping fat and muscle to shreds. In turn Tyran's men skewered and sliced at the fur and flesh of their attackers, heaping great chunks of bloodied meat to the floor with their sharpened blades and axes.

Marcii screamed as she ran, frantically trying to keep sight of Vixen as she was sprayed with blood and dashed with limbs and all other manner of vile bodily parts.

The young Dougherty caught fleeting images of wolves the size of bears, ferocious and terrifying, fighting a dozen and more men all at once, and indeed even winning.

They were colossal: impossibly so. And they seemed to be driven by something far beyond the realms of natural hunger.

There was much more fuel on the fire of this hunt than simply that.

It was a most unnatural sight.

Every man, woman and child that they killed, ripping them to shreds, tearing them limb from limb, the carcasses were instantly forgotten. Discarded without a hint of regard, the wolves moved immediately onto the next.

Darting down the centre of the street, cutting directly between a wolf and the three men urgently trying to fight it off, Marcii followed the young girl Vixen straight through it all, untouched by the carnage.

She darted right into an alleyway and Marcii followed, just about evading the hurtling body of an armoured enforcer as he was strewn down the street, followed immediately by an enormous wolf with fangs doused in blood.

Marcii screamed again and just about managed to dive out of the way, cutting and grazing her palms and legs as she threw herself into the alley, scraping along the floor on her own momentum.

Directly behind her the battered enforcer jumped to his feet and clubbed the bear sized wolf in the face with his hefty mace. But the huge brute just shrugged it off and wrapped his jaws around the man's head, drooling blood over him as the man's life poured down his scratched, battered armour.

Marcii, facing the wolf in terror, still on the floor, dragged herself slowly back. She tried not to make and sudden movements, but at the same time she was desperate to get away.

Eventually the demolished man's limbs just about stopped twitching and the wolf released his head from its massive, monstrous grasp.

His face was no longer recognisable, Marcii saw, as his body dropped limply to the floor.

Marcii's expression was the picture of desolation, but even as she stared at the horrific sight, she was unable to turn her eyes away. She felt drawn to it, almost as if she needed to watch.

Simultaneously though, even as she inescapably drank it in, Marcii's stomach turned violently and she threw up its contents onto the alleyway floor.

Barely able to control herself, once she'd heaved several times, Marcii looked back up nervously. She wiped her mouth and spat out the last remaining contents of her own vomit. The monstrosity of a creature turned its fearsome gaze upon her and she was filled all of a sudden with unrivalled dread.

She cursed at her own stupidity.

She shouldn't have stopped.

She should have followed Vixen like she was supposed to.

"Marcii!" Vixen screamed from behind her, as if on cue. "Marcii run!!" She cried desperately, but it was too late.

The terrified Dougherty threw a quick glance over her shoulder and saw Vixen at the other end of the narrow, dingy alleyway, with yet even more carnage unfolding in the street beyond where she stood.

Marcii turned and scrambled helplessly towards her young orphan, fleeing the enormous beast as it encroached awfully upon her.

Vixen urged her to run.

Marcii clambered desperately to her feet.

But then yet another figure appeared behind Vixen, looming at the other end of the alleyway in all its terrifying menace, armed to the hilt.

Marcii froze in her tracks.

Tyran.

"Looks like your time is up, witch." He breathed grittily down the narrow crevice of a street. His words dripped with gloating and carried somehow above the sound of every scream and every howl.

An unforgiving wind cut down between the tall, thin buildings. Though Marcii felt it, it barely touched her, for she was too filled with dread and horror.

Vixen leapt back down the alley in an instant, moving inhumanly fast, and crouched back at Marcii's side.

As ever her orphaned gaze was level and focused.

"Vixen…" Marcii breathed, but the young girl did not reply.

Her expression was set, as was she.

She was waiting to see who would make the first move.

The wolf.

Or Tyran.

The creature seemed a little warier now, for clearly it was uncertain about the figure approaching from the other end of the alleyway.

Nonetheless, they both still encroached in on the poor, helpless girls, ever further closing the gap between them and certain death.

"Vixen…" Marcii whispered again, terror in the tone.

But the young orphan merely stood on, steadfast and unmoving, as if she knew something that Marcii did not.

She always knew something that Marcii did not, it seemed.

"Hush…" Came Vixen's eventual and only reply, as the monstrous wolf and the dreadful Lord Tyran closed the cavity between them down to a mere dozen feet.

The houses on either side of the alley seemed taller and narrower than ever before and they pressed in around Marcii awfully, offering no escape.

The enormous wolf crouched, belly low to the ground, preparing to leap forward and claim its prey.

Tyran brandished his massive broadsword menacingly, smiling cruelly.

But even still, as ever, there was much more happening than met the eye.

Reaper made not a sound in the shifting darkness.

As he always would, he loomed dreadfully in the dead of the night.

Like a ghostly shadow he appeared directly behind the wolf, merging with the darkness itself, without a sight or smell or sound to be sensed.

Chapter Forty-Two

The wolf leapt from its crouch, launching itself through the air in a huge, arcing pounce.

In the same moment however, a massive, impending hand reached out from the darkness, moving with speed like lightning. Reaper's powerful grasp seized the wolf by the scruff of its neck, halting it in its tracks and dragging it back mid-flight.

Regardless of how enormous and powerful the wolf might have been, it seemed to have nothing on Reaper.

The monstrous, loving demon clutched the beast like a ragdoll.

The wolf squirmed and snarled and snapped at him, clawing his arm furiously. But it made not the slightest bit of difference.

Reaper drew his arm back in a single, enormous arc, even as the wolf barked and bit at him still.

He flung the beast forward with gargantuan might, launching it over Marcii and Vixen's heads and straight towards Tyran.

Adrenaline raced.

Howls echoed.

Time seemed to stand still and yet at the same time flit by in an instant.

"Now!!" Vixen screamed.

Tyran cried out, both with fury and with shock, as he found himself face to face with the furious, startled wolf. The beast hurtled through the air towards him with no control whatsoever over the course Reaper had set it on.

At the very last second the dreadful tyrant raised his blade in a final, futile defence, having no other way to shield himself.

Marcii found that she couldn't tear her eyes from the sight once again, but had no choice but to be whisked away as she felt herself ripped from the floor by Reaper's strong, warm hand.

She heard the sound of splitting ribs and bursting organs as Tyran's blade smashed through the wolf's ribcage, and indeed also his agonised cry as the beast slashed and bit instinctively at his face and body.

The sound carried off into the night, but then so did Marcii and Vixen, as Reaper scooped them up into his powerful arms and swept swiftly from the alleyway and back out into the streets.

Instantly they were met by yet more screams of terror as Reaper revealed himself in full to the townspeople.

But that couldn't be helped.

He ignored their cries and instead followed Vixen's directions without a moment's hesitation.

It was as if every word the girl spoke was gospel.

The young orphan pointed this way and that, screaming out instructions as she did so. The great hulking demon veered left and right through the streets flooded with carnage and blood.

"He's in there!!" Vixen suddenly yelled, shrieking above the sound of the slaughter and pointing directly at the building ahead, at the end of the street.

Reaper picked up somehow even more speed, if that were even possible, moving with power that Marcii had never before witnessed.

Midstride, the enormous demon shifted both girls onto one arm. Even as he ran still, Reaper raised his now free hand back and above his head, taking a giant, momentum filled swing.

He pummelled his fist into the side of the building that Vixen had indicated. His clenched hand hammered straight through the stone and mortar as if it were made from mere wood.

The wall shattered and exploded, spraying fragments of rock and shards of stone for a hundred feet in every direction, showering beast and man alike.

Reaper stepped back and Vixen and Marcii dove immediately and instinctively inside, scrambling without a thought through the massive hole Reaper had just created.

Marcii felt as if something altogether unknown had come over her as she drove her body forwards.

She had not a care in the world for herself, thinking only of Kaylm.

And then all of a sudden, like a rare, unrivalled gift, there he was.

Battered and bruised and barely even conscious, Kaylm was locked in what looked to be a purpose built cell.

Marcii had never seen anything like it.

Tyran had gone to great lengths to extend Kaylm's suffering, she noted lividly.

He was surrounded on three sides by sturdy, narrowly spaced metal bars, with a thick, barred door built into the front wall. He half leant and half lay up against the stone wall to which they were joined.

In the cell with him there was nothing but a rusty bucket.

The smell was horrendous.

Instinctively Marcii raced over to the cage that held her Kaylm, though, even if he had been free, she doubted he would have been able to get very far the state he was in.

She tugged desperately at the hefty bars, screaming his name as she did so, trying to rouse him from his ruined state. She rattled the door set into the cage in a frantic attempt to open it, but to no avail.

The bars didn't even budge.

The young Master Evans stirred slightly at the sound however.

"Marcii…?" He mumbled, unable to open his eyes and barely able to speak, for his face was so badly bruised and swollen: blue and purple and black.

Marcii ran back outside to Reaper and urged for him to help.

"Please get him out!!" She pleaded. "He's trapped, Reaper!!"

But the enormous demon only raised his hands and wove his reply silently into the air, pointing back towards the cage as he spoke.

Unbeknownst to Marcii, the young orphaned girl Vixen had stepped up to the bars surrounding Kaylm. She faced up against the sturdy, barred door and slowly wrapped her tiny fingers around their cold iron touch.

With the slightest, deftest of movements, Vixen wrenched her arms backwards and tore the door clean from the cell, ripping metal from metal with a horrendous grating, grinding sound.

As the bars buckled and the hinges broke clean off, churning with the sound of twisting iron and steel, the tiny girl tossed the door aside as if it were nothing at all. It smashed into the stone floor with a deafening metallic clang and she turned back to look at Marcii with an expression that was entirely unreadable.

But Marcii didn't even bother to stop in awe.

The time for that was long passed.

Even as Vixen tossed the door so casually and impossibly aside, Kaylm was somehow attempting to struggle to his feet.

He barely made it onto all fours. Every time he tried to stand he fell again, without a shadow of a doubt, though it wasn't for want of trying.

Over and over again he fought to stand.

Marcii dreaded to think how badly injured he was.

She imagined he was much worse that he looked.

But he was not one to give in easily.

Rushing in, she and Vixen helped him to his feet, as carefully and as quickly as they could manage.

Allowing Kaylm to hang off her shoulder, Marcii took his weight as much as she possibly could. Vixen supported him from the other side and together they helped him limp back through the hole in the wall that Reaper had created.

He scraped his feet over the rubble, unable to lift his legs properly. Reaper quickly cleared a walkway for them with a vast sweep of his arm to make it easier.

"We have to leave." Vixen warned. Her words were ominous and filled with more than a little disquiet. "We have to go now."

Almost immediately, as if on cue, new shouts sounded from down the street.

"There they are!!" Somebody yelled, pointing down the street towards Reaper with a long, thick blade.

All heads turned to bear their gazes down upon the witch and her demon. Suddenly, seemingly from the woodwork itself, there were a hundred and more of Tyran's men pouring towards them.

A spear flew through the air in a giant arc, launched by somebody shifting amongst the encroaching masses. Luckily, many of Tyran's men were still fighting the wolves, else Marcii and the others would surely have been overwhelmed.

The spear spun and hurtled and struck Reaper below the shoulder, threatening to bury itself down deep into his ribcage.

Luckily it barely touched him, glancing off his thick hide like a heavy raindrop. More spears followed though and a flurry of arrows arced obediently through the air in their wake.

Reaper turned to face his friends, shielding them from the raining attacks with his own body, as spears and arrows and even pitchforks spun off his hide relentlessly.

Soon, undoubtedly, Marcii feared that something would get through.

The swarming crowds were almost upon them.

Like a pounding heart flushing racing blood through an icy cold body, the freezing cold winds suddenly picked up and lashed at man and beast alike in the narrow streets.

Seizing his chance, Reaper scooped Marcii and Kaylm up into his arms, keeping them close to his chest, protecting them always.

Marcii screamed Vixen's name and craned her neck round to find the young orphan.

They could not leave her behind.

But Reaper's expression, as it always did, spoke a thousand words and more as Marcii squirmed to look back with searching eyes.

When she could not find Vixen, Marcii looked up to Reaper and realised all at once the hollowing truth.

Vixen was not coming.

She was gone.

Suddenly Marcii's eyes caught sight of something else: more arrows soaring yet again in high arcs through the air towards them.

Only this time, behind them the arrows streamed trails of black, billowing smoke, flaming furiously as they hurtled towards their targets.

"Reaper!!" Marcii screamed. "Look out!!"

Chapter Forty-Three

The flaming arrows rained down on Reaper's head and back as he stooped over Marcii and Kaylm, protecting them. He winced as they burned his shoulders, singing his fur and scalding his rough skin.

All of a sudden the closest of Tyran's men were upon them, brandishing swords and clubs and pitchforks.

Reaper saw them raise their weapons with an evil glint in their eyes and sprung explosively into action. Spinning and leaping all at once, the enormous demon ploughed directly through the approaching crowd, throwing people aside like ragdolls with his vast, tree trunk sized legs.

Without breaking his step Reaper took off at a dead run, hurtling down the street, moving too fast for even Marcii to keep track, let alone for anyone to halt him.

That didn't stop them from trying however, as both men and wolves threw themselves daringly into his monstrous path.

Hammering them with sweeping, one handed blows Reaper knocked the men harshly away, sending them flying two dozen feet and more, over and through buildings without a care.

The wolves proved to be a tougher challenge, as they bared their vengeful, dripping teeth. But Reaper didn't stop to think on their threats, idle only to him. He simply battered them with his massive fist as he ran through them, burying their heads into the cobblestones, smashing and shattering their feeble skulls.

He was far too focused to allow anything to stop him.

Fuelled by sheer, demonic adrenaline, he was getting Marcii and Kaylm out, and nothing was going to stand in his way.

It was as simple as that.

Almost before she knew it, Marcii glanced back as the icy cold wind whipped her hair about her face and saw that the lights and the screams and the howls of the Newmarket slaughter were far behind them.

Reaper swept through the darkness of the still early morning wilderness.

The sun was slowly rising on the horizon far to the east, creeping its head over the hills and lighting their way with glorious orange and red and golden rays.

Marcii continued to look on, filled with a great, swirling mix of emotions. The sorry sight of the market town that had once been her home lit up the black sky with blazing firelight.

Flames ate at buildings, presumably in an attempt to drive the wolves away, and the screams echoed through the night even still.

It was not the same place it had once been.

Once upon a time Marcii had called Newmarket home.

But after all that had happened, she never would again.

Now, as far as the young Dougherty was concerned, it was a forsaken place, torn apart by the ensuing war.

Ruined, like so many other things, by the Dreadhunt.

Chapter Forty-Four

Reaper ran at a dead sprint for nearly three hours, maintaining a speed that was quite simply impossible, ludicrous in fact.

Nonetheless, he did it anyway.

Carrying the accused pair protectively in his warm embrace all the while, he scooped them close in his arms like children.

Finally, after the great demon had covered many miles, and indeed also once Marcii had had ample opportunity to let sink in the gravity and immense weight of everything that had happened, he slowed his breakneck pace.

Reducing his stride gradually to a run, then a jog, and eventually to a vast lope, ducking beneath the dense canopy, Reaper wove his way into the thick patch of woodlands he had been aiming for.

It was much darker amongst the trees and immediately Marcii felt her enormous friend's relief flooding from him as he merged into the heavy shadows.

Deeper and deeper into the woodlands Reaper carried them, winding his way through the trees expertly, venturing as far as he could out of sight and out of mind.

When he felt that he'd gone far enough, however far that might have been, Marcii didn't know, Reaper finally wound to a halt.

The young Dougherty jumped down from his arm and he laid Kaylm carefully down upon the soft, mossy ground at the base of a stout oak tree.

Immediately Marcii set to work dressing Kaylm and Reaper's wounds. She had only very limited provisions and resorted once again to mud for Reaper's burns.

She could not use that to treat Kaylm though. Instead, with help from her demonic friend, Marcii managed to find an ice cold brook that babbled through the dense trees. The water did not bring miracles, but it certainly helped.

Marcii managed to clean Kaylm up considerably. He even came to for just long enough to take a drink through his dreadfully swollen lips.

He soon fell into unconsciousness again though, and Reaper insisted that Marcii rest too.

It had been an awfully long night and she had barely rested since the night before.

He knew she was exhausted.

Complying, Marcii laid her head down beside Kaylm's on the moss, just a few feet from where Reaper sat up against the towering oak tree.

A harsh wind cut through the sea of trunks that Marcii hadn't noticed before whilst she'd been busy tending to her friends.

It whistled annoyingly as it barraged them and seeped cruelly through the ocean of bark.

Away from Reaper, having just spent so many hours in his arms, immediately Marcii felt the harsh grasp of the wind cutting through her.

"Oh stop it!" She muttered under her breath without thinking, turning away from the gust and shuffling closer still to Kaylm.

She was so tired that the young Dougherty was asleep in moments.

Far too quickly to notice that the wind died in an instant, as if on her command.

Of course, Reaper was not asleep, for that was something he needed not, and he most certainly did notice.

The enormous demon's expression spoke a thousand and more different things all at once. Most prominently of all though, it showed quite clearly how profound that moment seemed to be, whether Marcii had noticed it or not.

He looked on respectfully at the young Dougherty.

He smiled with great care for her, as he always did. His eyes however were filled with something else.

Something that resembled an even greater understanding.

Hopefully, in time, it would be an understanding that Marcii in turn would share.

He could feel the time approaching, drawing nearer by the moment. There were too many traces of it to be very far off.

All he could do was continue on.

But he was patient as ever.

Soon she would also discover what he'd come to realise. Or, perhaps more likely, what he'd known all along.

Either way, it didn't really matter.

The time was drawing near.
There wasn't long to wait now.
But wait he would.

Chapter Forty-Five

The day drew out, long and clear and quiet as Marcii rested.

Nightfall eventually came and the young Dougherty stirred into wakefulness, accompanied too by Kaylm as he roused. He was young and strong and determined and, though his body was gravely damaged, he was recovering quickly.

As Marcii awakened she saw that Reaper had not moved even an inch since she'd fallen asleep. She smiled warmly up at the monstrous demon who had watched over them so caringly while they'd slept.

His expression was mixed however, she noted critically.

He looked to be lost in thought, as if he was considering something so deeply rooted and significant that there were simply no words to explain it.

Emerging from the treeline, heading westerly once more, Reaper scooped Marcii and the now conscious Kaylm into his arms, setting off at a steady pace.

The air that night wasn't just icy cold, it was bitter and harsh. Gnawing at Marcii's exposed face and fingers, it bit at her skin relentlessly.

She looped one hand into Kaylm's almost without thinking. Interlocking her fingers with his she squeezed tightly, taking comfort from his touch.

Marcii felt safe and content knowing the three of them were going home, and that finally, at long last, they would be safe.

As ever, little did she know.

Occasionally the winds picked up, repeatedly barraging the three of them as they went. Every time though, yet again, Marcii quelled the elements with barely more than a whim.

Amidst all of that, Marcii spent hours staring up at the stars in the blanket of coal that lay above her. She stroked the back of Kaylm's hand with her thumb, their fingers still entwined whilst he intermittently dozed and recuperated.

The night drew on and over time clouds swarmed in and shrouded Marcii's view of the lifeless, thriving ocean above.

She frowned a little in disappointment and immediately the clouds parted and revealed the treasures they had concealed from her once more.

Somehow, though it had been of her own doing, Marcii barely even noticed the unbelievable feat she'd just undertaken. She merely smiled peacefully and settled even deeper into Reaper's thick fur, rubbing Kaylm's hand continuously as she gazed wistfully up at all those other worlds once again.

Reaper's expression turned imploring, though Marcii did not notice in the darkness.

Usually, beneath the moonshine and stargaze so bright, Reaper would have been concerned that his silhouette was too obvious in the night.

However, seeing Marcii's contentedness, without even realising herself what she'd done, Reaper simply pressed on, taking the chance.

To say that these unbelievable feats Marcii was performing were significant wouldn't even have come close to the truth.

Tomorrow would be the day, Reaper decided.

He didn't know exactly what would happen.

Had he done, he would have been overjoyed beyond belief.

As it stood though, even still he thought only of Marcii.

Eventually the young Dougherty slept. Subconsciously she pulled the clouds back in again and knitted them together to conceal the three of them as they crossed the canyon and the fields and the rolling hills in the dark of the night, making as ever for the shelter of the abandoned, ghostly citadel Ravenhead.

None of them knew what was waiting for them however, and it would surely prove to be more astonishing than any of them could possibly imagine.

Chapter Forty-Six

Sunrise encompassed the land, beckoning the day in a desperate, longing sort of way. The shadowy blanket hovering above half the world gave way to a lush, sapphire ocean filled with birdsong and wind chill.

It was the first time Marcii had heard any animal calls whilst she'd been in Ravenhead, though whether that was noteworthy or not, she didn't know. She didn't see the birds however, and the thought of them slipped just as quickly from her mind as it had come.

Kaylm seemed to have recovered considerably. Though his body was still bruised and battered and cut all over, once he'd eaten, probably more than he'd been fed in days, he seemed immediately stronger.

Even managing to find his feet, for he felt his will returning in great flurries, Kaylm walked with Marcii for a short while. In the early morning sunlight through the still abandoned streets of Ravenhead they roamed.

At first they didn't speak, for it seemed there were no words for what they needed to say.

They simply held hands as they wandered, oblivious for a time as to the momentous change that Ravenhead had undertaken in their absence.

As of yet, though Reaper sensed that something was amiss, even he hadn't fully comprehended what was happening.

Aside from the chirping birdsong, all was quiet. Reaper could not settle however and he found himself cutting from street to street, looking for something, though he had no idea exactly what.

Eventually, after having missed each other at least a dozen times, Marcii and Kaylm's path crossed Reaper's.

They all stopped abruptly.

None of them spoke.

Marcii's eyes found Reaper's, deep like jet black coal. She saw they were filled with something that she too could feel.

Something was happening.

Or had already happened.

They weren't sure which, as neither of them could put their finger on it.

Suddenly, out of the corner of her eye, a flicker of movement caught Marcii's eye.

In reality there had been no movement at all: but that's exactly what had drawn Marcii's attention.

Reaper and Kaylm followed her gaze and the enormous demon even managed to look shocked, wondering how she'd sensed it before him.

Perhaps as expected, Marcii's eyes found their way up to Raven's Keep, settling heavily upon the tower and staying there.

Of the three of them, Kaylm's expression was the most confused.

But then, that was only natural.

He was the only one unable to sense what Reaper and Marcii could both feel.

"What is it?" Kaylm asked, keeping his voice low, though he wasn't sure what made him whisper.

At first Marcii didn't reply, and when she eventually did her voice too was hushed.

"Up there." She breathed.

Reaper nodded slowly, but other than that neither of them moved.

Kaylm wanted to speak, but felt for a moment for some reason as if he shouldn't. As if the words were forbidden.

Eventually though, not knowing any better, the young Master Evans eventually breathed his next question.

"What is it?" He asked. "Should we go up?"

Marcii looked at him for a moment as if she couldn't believe he'd asked that question, and perhaps more to the point that she hadn't thought of it herself.

Their footsteps were slow and cautious as the three of them ascended Raven's Keep. Reaper's strides were long and seemed to be in slow motion. As Marcii and Kaylm followed him their hearts were filled all the while with uncertainty.

The room at the top of the staircase was as wide and round and desolate as ever, all except for one small detail.

Raven was waiting for them as they appeared, looking on at them with her aged, luminescent violet eyes. Marcii and Reaper's gazes both fell upon her, whilst, just as before, Kaylm's eyes passed straight through her.

Instead, Kaylm's gaze fell immediately upon the other figure waiting for them at the top of the tower: the only one he could see, and his mouth dropped open when he saw her.

"Malorie!?" He gasped, shocked at the sight.

Marcii saw her too, though she wasn't sure for some bizarre reason whether she'd been expecting her or not.

The mysterious woman's expression was filled with a profound mix of emotions, revealing everything that she felt in her own bright, violet eyes, churned together all at once.

But she was dead.

Why only Marcii and Reaper could see Raven, the young Dougherty didn't know.

The fact that Kaylm could see Malorie and not Raven was unnerving.

It was perhaps proof that Malorie was real and Raven was not.

Unbelievably, she had survived the river.

Somehow she had escaped.

And now, impossibly, she was here.

Alive.

This couldn't have happened.

It just wasn't possible.

Regardless, it had happened anyway.

The look on Reaper's face was a sight beyond description.

Without a word Malorie rushed forwards and Reaper swept her up into his arms joyously.

He scooped the unbelievable woman into his loving embrace, encompassing her tiny frame completely. His deep, jet black coal eyes were filled with more love than Marcii had ever seen in her life.

The expressions on both their faces didn't need interpreting, for it was clear as day that Malorie and Reaper meant the absolute world to each other.

Marcii's hand unconsciously found Kaylm's as they looked on in awed, respectful silence.

She had not expected this.

Any of it.

Reaper held Malorie still, pulling the peculiar, murdered woman so close that the young Dougherty thought he might never let her go.

Clearly there was much here that she knew nothing of.

The ghostly figure of Raven looked on with an expression all of her own, for clearly she had seen much of this before.

It brought to her mind memories of happiness, filling her eyes with glorious delight. But, at the same time, her gaze was tinted with sorrow and regret.

Raven's eyes revealed the truth of memories so excruciating that it was unbearable. There were simply not enough years in the world for them to be recalled without pain, let alone for her to relive them as she was now having to.

Even so, time waits for no one.

The very sight that could have brought back such surging emotions had just unfolded before her, bringing a whole new meaning to her longing, otherworldly existence.

Chapter Forty-Seven

Was Malorie really a witch?

And if she wasn't, how in the world could she still be alive?

Was she the one responsible for all that had happened?

All the hunts?

All the torture?

All the executions?

Marcii didn't know what to think anymore.

She had never even believed in witches, regardless of the fact she'd spent the latter part of her life being hunted for being one.

Naturally, Kaylm felt the same way, although he'd watched Malorie drown in the river with his own eyes, just as Marcii had done.

Whether she'd realised it or not though, Marcii had been growing used to the supernatural over the past weeks, months even. It was something that, even subconsciously, she had been swiftly coming to terms with.

Reaper eventually placed Malorie down, though he seemed more than just a little reluctant to let her go.

All the while the enormous demon's hand stretched out and Malorie gripped his massive fingers in her tender, delicate palms, unwilling to lose his touch for even a moment.

The mysterious woman turned her gaze once more upon the young Dougherty. Her eyes said just as much as Reaper's always did, if not even more.

It was as if she could see or sense something most profound, and that indeed also there was an immense, intolerable sadness linked to that knowledge.

Her eyes were more violet and more luminous than ever before and the emotion housed within them was barely concealed, flowing endlessly. They spoke to Marcii with a thousand heeds of warning. Seeing them, the young Dougherty knew immediately there was infinitely more going on here than she could possibly hope to imagine.

So much had happened in such a short space of time, yet it seemed as though she'd still barely even scratched the surface.

Her mind simply could not piece together how Malorie fitted in to all of this, for undoubtedly it was more deeply and more intricately than she could possibly ever begin to comprehend.

And then there was Vixen, and Raven too.

The young, abandoned orphan who, quite clearly, wasn't what she appeared to be. And the ghost of a woman whom Marcii knew even less about than she did Vixen.

The intricacies here were simply too great for Marcii to fathom in that moment.

But then came Malorie's words.

When she spoke, her heavy voice was thick with emotion and laden with promise of yet more suffering to come, only disturbing Marcii further.

"We must find the old man Midnight." The mysterious woman instructed.

Glancing between the young Dougherty and the ghostly figure of Raven, she spoke just as much with her bright violet eyes as she did with her tongue, filling the air with fresh dread that had never before existed in Marcii's mind.

As is the nature of such things.

"He is in grave danger." Malorie warned, her words ominous and foreboding. "Only he holds the key to stop all this madness."

Thank you for reading Reaper
Book Two of The Dreadhunt Trilogy

I hope you enjoyed it

Look out for

Midnight
Book Three of The Dreadhunt Trilogy

Marcii finds herself yet again upon the dreadful streets of Newmarket, seemingly unable to escape them. Having been forced to return upon the witch Malorie's will, she and her companions are in search of the old man Midnight, who somehow might hold the key to their salvation from the Dreadhunt.

When the old man admits that indeed he is not what he seems, an entirely new world opens up to Marcii: one that she could never even have imagined. Those responsible for the savage attacks in Newmarket reveal themselves once and for all, stepping hauntingly from the shadows.

It soon becomes clear to the young Dougherty that these events were not as they first seemed. But the more she manages to unravel the truth, the deeper Marcii finds that she herself is entwined within it.

Ross Turner

You may also enjoy

The Redwoods - Book One

Young Vivian Featherstone comes from a long line of
Lords and Ladies, and her family's seat of
unquestionable influence, wealth and power is owed
to a much treasured heirloom, passed down from
generation to generation.
But when little Vivian, only eleven years of age,
narrowly escapes a plot by a rival, feuding family to
eliminate the Featherstones, she finds herself lost in
the mysterious Redwood Forest.
With assassins pursuing her, and strange and
dangerous creatures all around, can Vivian survive?
And will she discover the power of her family's
heirloom before it's too late?

The Redwoods Rise and Fall - Book Two

Vivian has returned to Virtus, she has defeated the
Greystones, and the once great city even seems to be
well on the way to recovery. But something isn't
right. Vivian feels stranded amongst all that she has
fought to gain, and suffered so terribly to lose. And
now it seems there are new threats and dangers,
stemming from old evils. Just as all those before her
have either succeeded or succumbed, now she too
must face her own rise and fall.

Or

Voices in the Mirror

Evening encroached upon them and a deep, vast, endless darkness swept in upon the tiny, insignificant village of Riverbrook.

Cold winds cut through the trees and bit harshly at the exposed faces of anybody who dared still remain out under the enormous sky, scattered with an ocean of burned out stars that seethed and watched without a sound.

A million and more shining eyes that had gazed down upon the face of the Earth for a hundred millennia and even longer, turned their cruel eyes now to all that was unfolding before them, and for not the first time in history, something impossible and wonderful, a miracle, began to unfold.

Please visit my facebook and twitter pages for the latest updates

Ross Turner Books
@RossTurnerBooks

www.rossturnerbooks.com

19624608R00152

Printed in Great Britain
by Amazon